I pick a piece of paper out of the hat. I'm so excited that I can barely unfold it.

Good gravy in the navy.

The longer I stare at the letters written in green ink on that little piece of paper, the bigger her name gets. My voice flat-out refuses to say what my eyes already know.

"Mya, who is your Spirit Week partner?" asks Mrs. Davis.

I try to tell her. "It's . . . I pulled . . ."

Skye grabs my arm and reads the paper, then bursts out laughing.

"Mya got Mean Connie Tate!"

Also by Crystal Allen

How Lamar's Bad Prank Won a Bubba-Sized Trophy

The Laura Line

The Magnificent Mya Tibbs: The Wall of Fame Game

The MAGNIFICENT Mya Tibbs

SPIRIT
WEEK
SHOWDOWN

CRYSTAL ALLEN

Illustrations by Eda Kaban

BALZER + BRAY

An Imprint of HarperCollinsPublishers

Balzer + Bray is an imprint of HarperCollins Publishers.

Spirit Week Showdown: The Magnificent Mya Tibbs
Text copyright © 2016 by Crystal Allen
Illustrations copyright © 2016 by Eda Kaban
For information address HarperCollins Children's Books,
a division of HarperCollins Publishers,
195 Broadway, New York, NY 10007.

www.harpercollinschildrens.com

Library of Congress Cataloging-in-Publication Data
Library of Congress Cataloging-in-Publication Data
Allen, Crystal.
Spirit week showdown / Crystal Allen ; illustrated by Eda Kaban.
— First edition.
    pages   cm — (The Magnificent Mya Tibbs ; 1)
Summary: Nine-year-old Mya is excited about participating in
School Spirit Week, even making a pinky promise with her best friend
Naomi to be her partner, but when she accidentally gets paired with the
biggest bully in school, Mean Connie, Naomi is mad at Maya for breaking
her promise, so she must learn to work with Mean Connie and try and get
her friend back.
    ISBN 978-0-06-234234-8
    [1.   Friendship—Fiction. 2.   Promises—Fiction. 3.   Schools—
Fiction.]   I. Kaban, Eda, illustration.   II. Title.
PZ7.A42527Sp   2016   2015015384
[Fic]—dc23   CIP
                                                                     AC

Typography by Carla Weise
17 18 19 20   BVG   10 9 8 7 6
❖
First paperback edition, 2017

To all of my nieces.
I love you to pieces.

Chapter One

I'm only wearing five braids to school today. I usually wear nine because that's how old I am. But this week I'm counting down the days to Spirit Week using my hair instead of a calendar. On Tuesday I had seven braids. Yesterday, six. When I get to one, it'll be time for Spirit Week!

I push both feet into my cowgirl boots without sitting down just like I've seen real cowgirls do, then decorate my wrist with the yellow bracelet I made last night. My posters of Annie Oakley and Cowgirl Claire seem to root for me as I *ka-clunk* around in my boots, pretending to lasso the cows and horses that Dad painted on my walls. One day I'll be on a poster too, as the first jewelry-making, calf-roping cowgirl from Bluebonnet, Texas.

Dad even put different words to that song "She'll Be Comin' 'Round the Mountain When She Comes" just for me! I grab an imaginary microphone and sing as if I'm in a concert.

"She'll be ropin' all the cattle when she comes!
Ruby gems and yellow diamonds on her thumbs.
Mya Tibbs is such a winner,
Because winning is what's in 'er.
She'll be ropin' all the cattle when she comes!"

Knock, knock.

I drop the mike, open the door, and frown. It's my brother. His real name is Micah, but I call him Nugget because his skin is brown and his head is shaped like a chunk of chicken. He thinks I named him after a piece of gold.

"This better be important," I say.

He puts a finger to his lips. "Shh. I need a favor."

He's got a copy of the *Bluebonnet Tribune* stuck between his armpit and his ribs. I think he's the only fifth grader on the planet who reads the paper before breakfast.

"I have a meeting at the park this morning with Solo Grubb. It's about Spirit Week."

I roll my eyes. "So what's the favor?"

"Shh!" he says again. His face has worry in it, so I lose my frown and listen as he whispers like we're in church. "I can't walk with you all the way to school today. Don't tell, or I'll get grounded, okay?"

I think about the time I tried to swing across the dining-room table on the ceiling fan and pulled it clean out of the ceiling. We were out of glue, so Nugget used toothpaste to put it back up, but it fell down in the middle of dinner and smashed Mom's meat loaf. He took the blame.

"I won't tell," I say.

He grins and then gives me a little shove on the shoulder. That's his way of saying thanks. I shove him back. That's how I say you're welcome.

He hands me the newspaper. "Looks like Naomi Jackson won the pageant last night."

She looks beautiful. To think, my best friend is Junior Miss Lone Star!

Nugget snatches the paper back. "Come

on—enough staring at her picture. I smell pancakes. Last one to the table eats Mom's sandwich," he says, racing me downstairs.

"Ugh! That's gross!" I say, running as fast as I can to beat him.

Mom's got a thing for the color red, and it shows all over our kitchen. We've got red pots, red dishcloths, a red stove, and a red refrigerator. She even shuffles around in red house slippers shaped like cowgirl boots. Nugget and I bought them for her when she stopped wearing real ones. I guess it's hard to *ka-clunk* when you're going to burp out a baby in a month.

Nugget bows. "Greetings and salutations, my lady."

Mom curtsies. "Good morning, Sir Nugget," she says, eating a peanut butter–and–onion sandwich. Since she's been pregnant, Mom wants onions on everything.

I give her a hug. "How are you feeling?"

She rubs her belly. "Oh Mya, the baby kicked all night, and I'm so hungry all the time."

I cover my nose. "You know, onions are really evil unicorn eyeballs. If you don't stop eating them, our new baby might grow a horn in the middle of her forehead."

4

Mom's eyebrows rise. "That sounds like a tara-diddle to me."

We both grin. Taradiddles are what cowgirls call good traveling stories. They're different from lies or fibs because taradiddles aren't meant to hurt anybody. The real reason I want Mom to stop eating those nasty sandwiches is because it makes her breath smell like the big green Dumpster at our school. But I would never say that to her face.

Dad walks by with a cup of coffee and pulls out his chair. "Morning, everybody. Nugget, I need you and Mya to help out at the store on Saturday. Before we leave we'll have to load Buttercup onto the back of the truck."

Buttercup is a mechanical bull that Dad keeps in the backyard until he needs it at the store for things like sales or concert promotions.

Nugget stabs a piece of pancake. "But tomorrow we find out who our Spirit Week partners are going to be. I've got plans for the whole weekend. See, there's this guy, Solo . . ."

Dad gives Nugget *the look*, the one that means "What part of 'I need you at the store' did you not understand?" My brother's eyes drop to his plate of pancakes.

"What's going on at the store, Dad? Are we

getting a bunch of new stuff?" I ask.

Dad owns Tibbs's Farm and Ranch Store on Main Street. His great-great-grandfather started the store. It kept getting handed down, and now it belongs to Dad. I thought hand-me-downs only happened with clothes and boots.

Dad nods. "Bronco Buck Willis canceled for the Fall Festival rodeo. Now I've got to send back all of those Bronco Buck items I special ordered. Sure hope I can get a refund."

Mom shuffles over, pours Dad more coffee, and kisses him on the cheek. I drop my fork and frown. This is no time for kissing.

"Bronco Buck canceled on us? And he's not even that good! You should've gotten Cowgirl Claire. She's the best calf roper on the planet—and she'd never back out on a promise."

Dad shrugs. "The festival committee is trying to find somebody to replace him."

"I hope whoever they get is awesome, because I'm going to win VIP tickets to the Fall Festival, and I don't want to waste front-row seats on a terrible roper," I say.

Dad chuckles. "Where on earth can you win those?"

I run around to Dad and hold his face with both

of my hands as I look him in the eyes. "Listen to this, Dad, you're not going to believe it. Principal Winky is giving away VIP tickets to the best Spirit Week partners in each grade. I'm talking free food, front-row tickets to the shows, but best of all, you get to be first in line for all of the rides!" I let go of his face.

Dad's eyebrows rise. "Holy moly! So it's like a contest? Winners get VIP tickets?"

"You got it," says Nugget, giving Dad two thumbs up.

I grab my backpack. "And winning is exactly what I plan to do. See you guys later!"

On our way to school, I show Nugget my bracelet. "What do you think?"

He glances at my wrist. "The composition is impressive."

"Thanks," I say, even though I have no idea what *composition* means.

Two boys dash by on bikes. They're both in Nugget's class. One points at my brother. "Look! It's Word Nerd Nugget and his sister, Cowgirl Mya!"

Nugget balls up his fists. "Stop calling me that! I mean it!"

"Don't listen to them," I say. "They're just mad because you're the Wizard of Words. So why are you talking to Solo about Spirit Week anyway? Isn't Fish your Spirit Week partner?"

Nugget holds up a finger, then smiles. "Yes, but I have a theory. It involves Solo Grubb. If my theory works, I won't get called Word Nerd Nugget anymore. Maybe I'll even get picked to play basketball."

My nose wrinkles as I think about what's happened to him in the past. "Every time you try to shoot hoops at recess, you end up in the nurse's office. Is Solo going to teach you how to play? Are you and Solo good friends already?" I ask.

"Not yet," says Nugget. "But I've been calculating the possibilities of Solo and me becoming best friends during Spirit Week. The odds are significantly high. I'm factoring in—"

I snap at him. "*Best* friend? No way. Solo Grubb is rude and thinks he's the coolest guy on the planet. You're nothing like Solo, and you hardly even know him."

Nugget snaps back. "How long did you know Naomi Jackson before she became your best friend? She's been at our school less than a month. Solo's been here since kindergarten. At least Solo and I both like basketball. What do you and Naomi have in common?"

I grab my brother's backpack strap and then

deadeye him. "We've got lots in common. We both like jewelry; we like the twins, Starr and Skye; we like our teacher, Mrs. Davis; we both like the color red; and we like being best friends." I hold up a finger. "Plus, we both want those Fall Festival VIP tickets, and we're going to get them."

Chapter Two

I could have given Nugget a bunch more reasons why Naomi and I are best friends. It's not because Dairy Queen writes *Congratulations, Naomi Jackson* right above their Blizzard specials every time she wins a beauty pageant, or because she does car commercials on TV with her dad.

She's the only person at school who knows that I use my braids as a calendar. Some kids might think that's silly, but Naomi doesn't. She even pinkie promised that she wouldn't tell anyone just to make sure no one laughs at me. She's awesome at keeping promises. So am I.

I remember the day she asked me, "You want to be best friends?" I swallowed my answer and choked right there in the hall. Once I stopped coughing, I said "Yes."

That was only twenty-two days ago, but I think we were born to be best friends.

"Hey Nugget, Mya, wait up!"

It's Fish, waving his arms in the air to get our attention.

"Don't say anything to him about my meeting with Solo," says Nugget.

Fish's backpack bounces up and down as he runs. He fist-bumps Nugget and then me.

"Hiya, Mya Papaya! Happy Aardvark Day! Did you know aardvarks are fast diggers?"

I love it when he calls me Mya Papaya. It's not a giddy-up-cowgirl name like Cowgirl Claire or Annie Oakley, but it's good enough for me. I give him a big smile.

"Hi, Fish! Nope, I had no idea." I ask my brother, "Did you?"

Nugget shrugs, shakes his head, and rolls his eyes like we're bothering him. "I read that somewhere. They eat ants and termites just like anteaters. No big deal."

Fish has one of those weird holiday calendars.

If something is celebrated anywhere on the planet, Nugget and Fish celebrate it, too.

Fish turns around so he can walk backward and face Nugget as he talks. "Did you read about aardvarks in that *Safari Journal* newsletter or was it in the *Animal Education* magazine? Geez, Nugget, you're a walking computer. You must have two brains. One for input, one for output!"

Nugget doesn't smile. "I'm not weird. I've got one brain just like everybody else."

I glance at my brother. I can tell he's still angry with those boys on the bikes, but he shouldn't take it out on his best friend.

Fish's real name is Homer Leatherwood. His dad named him that because he loves baseball. He has eyes bluer than the sky, but they are belly-whopper, bullfrog huge. His curly blond hair sits high like the bubbles in my bathtub. He's Nugget's best friend, but Fish is one of my favorite people, too, because he's always nice to me.

"I can't believe all of the stuff we'll get with those VIP tickets! I can see myself getting free funnel cakes and buffalo burgers," says Fish.

"Last year I wasn't tall enough for all the good rides," I say. "But I am now!"

"Don't forget front-row seats and backstage

passes for all the shows," says Nugget.

I pretend I'm roping a calf. "Including the rodeo!"

Fish rubs his hands together. "Nugget, we're going to be fifth-grade VIPs!"

I hold up a finger. "Naomi and I are going to be the fourth-grade winners!"

We stop at the corner and wait for the crossing guard's signal. My brother stares across the street. "There he is! Hey, Solo, over here!"

Inside the park fence, a boy swishes a shot. He has brown skin and shiny black hair, and he wears expensive basketball shoes. He waves. I wave back, even though I've never met him.

"He's good," I say.

My brother laughs. "He's not just good. Solo's boo-yang good. Fish, you know Solo?"

Fish spits in the grass. "You mean the kid who thinks he's cooler than ice?"

"He's not just cool. He's boo-yang cool," says Nugget, looking across the street.

Fish rolls his eyes and then looks at me. "He's not boo-yang cool."

The smile slides off of Nugget's face. "That's your opinion."

TWEEEEET! The crossing guard stops all traffic. Nugget gives me a friendly shove and a smile.

"I'm crossing here. Catch up with you later."

Fish and I watch Nugget run inside the park and high-five Solo. I keep my lips zipped because Nugget asked me not to tell Fish about his secret Spirit Week meeting. I worry about how Fish is going to feel when he finds out what Nugget is doing.

"You're his best friend, Fish," I say.

Fish is still watching Nugget and Solo. "Yeah, I'm still his best friend."

To me, Nugget can't win Spirit Week without Fish. Best friends make awesome Spirit Week partners, and I'll prove it when Naomi and I win those fourth-grade VIP tickets.

Fish opens the school door and lets me walk in first. "See you at lunch, Mya," he says.

"Happy Aardvark Day," I yell as he rushes down the hall.

Everywhere I look there are posters and signs about Spirit Week. My favorite is the one with two cowboys sitting on horses. One says "Howdy, Partner." The other cowboy says, "I'm not just a partner. I'm your Spirit Week partner! Yee-haw!"

I spot Naomi near the water fountain, surrounded by boys and girls congratulating her on winning the pageant, and she thanks them with a smile.

When I reach her, she touches my braids. "Your

hair's so cute today. Where's Nugget?"

I point toward the school door. "He'll be here in a few minutes."

Last year, I had two friends, Skye and Starr Falling. We were just regular girls. But now, we're popular because of Naomi, and I'm *mega*popular since she's my best friend. Soon Nugget shows up, sweaty and out of breath. "Greetings and salutations."

Naomi plays with her hair and smiles at my brother. "Hi, Golden Nugget."

I frown. "Why'd you call him that?"

Naomi shrugs. "He told me his first name is Golden."

I glare at my brother. "Chicken is more like it."

He grins. "Just call me Nugget. See you at lunch, Mya."

Naomi watches him jog down the hall. "Are you sure he doesn't have a girlfriend?"

I roll my eyes. "Maybe Godzilla, but I think she broke up with him."

She laughs. "You're so funny, Mya. We better get to class."

One of the best things about being in fourth grade is our classroom. It has an extra room near Mrs. Davis's desk. She calls it our adjoining room. We call it awesome! This extra room has a rainbow-shaped door with "The Cubby Cave" written above it. We just call it the Cave, because no fourth grader in their right mind would use the word "cubby." Inside the Cave, each of us has a long wooden cabinet with our name on it. They look like lockers only way better because they have tons of space and they're all different colors instead of the ugly gray ones they have in middle school.

Inside each cabinet, there's a square at the top for books, a hook for our coat and backpack, and a drawer at the bottom for supplies and lunchboxes. It's boo-yang cool, and a fun place to hang out before the bell rings. By the time Naomi and I get to our cabinets, the place is packed with our classmates.

Suddenly the Cave goes from rock-concert loud to dead-people quiet. Students freeze. Even the air conditioner cuts off. I'm scared to look, but I have to know what's happening. A tall girl, taller than most teachers, stands next to me. I slowly back away from my cabinet.

It's Mean Connie Tate.

There are fifteen rumors about Mean Connie, and all of them are true. Rumors like breaking her brother's fingers, stealing boots off a homeless lady, and trashing the Bluebonnet Bakery because she ordered chocolate doughnuts and they accidentally gave her lemon filled.

She glares at Naomi. "Get your grimy hands off my door."

"I hope I didn't get any of your bully germs on me," says Naomi.

It only takes two seconds for the Cave to empty. I'd leave, too, if Naomi wasn't my best friend, because it's going to get ugly in here. I think there's going to be blood. Lots of blood.

Mean Connie steps closer to Naomi. "Stay away from me, Jackson."

Naomi shrugs but doesn't seem scared at all. "You stay away from me, too!"

Mean Connie gets her books and stomps out of the Cave. Naomi and I wait for her to get far enough away before we talk.

"Are you okay? She really scares me," I say.

Naomi rolls her eyes. "We used to go to the same private school in second grade. Mean Connie tried to bully me, but I told on her and she got kicked out."

Naomi holds her cell phone up high. "Before we walk into class, let's take a picture for my portfolio in case I ever need one of me and my best friend in the Cave on a Thursday."

I put my face to hers and we smile so big that it takes up the whole picture screen. *Click*.

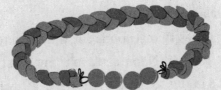

Chapter Three

Mrs. Davis makes us sit boy, girl, boy, girl, because she thinks that will stop us from talking. She's right. Even the twins have a boy between them. Michael Silsbee sits in front of me. He's got big ears and hears everything, but he talks about as much as my stuffed animals, which means not at all. Kenyan Tayler sits behind me, and I wouldn't talk to him if he was the last boy on earth because he's always pulling my braids. I *ka-clunk* over to Naomi's desk with her.

"I love your vest, Mya," she says.

I look down at it. "Annie Oakley wore one just

like it. Cowgirl Claire has one, too."

Naomi frowns. "Who are they? What grade are they in? I don't think I've met them."

I giggle. "They're famous cowgirls."

Mom bought my vest at Billy Bob's dollar store, even though I tell everyone she got it in the gift shop at the Cowgirl Hall of Fame. There's only one teeny-weeny difference between the two. I bet all the labels inside the vests at the gift shop say *Made with Genuine Cowhide*. Billy Bob's label just says *size small*.

I point toward the door. "Here come the twins."

I've been friends with Starr and Skye Falling since first grade. I'm not sure where they came from. They just showed up in class one day like aliens, and for the longest time, that's what I thought they were. The longer I knew them, the more I believed it. I'd never call them that to their faces, but there is so much proof.

Why else would Mr. and Mrs. Falling name their twins Starr and Skye unless they fell down to Earth from another planet?

They are always together and never disagree.

They eat the same foods, dance the same way, and wear matching outfits.

They both have blond hair, blond eyebrows,

freckles, little noses, and tiny lips.

If one gets in trouble and cries, the other one cries, too.

Two weeks later, I found out their parents opened the Bluebonnet Hunting Gear and Observatory, in between Dad's store and the Burger Bar, home of the Cobb burger. That burger is gross. It's a hamburger with eggs, coleslaw, onions, barbecue sauce, and beans right on the bun! Since she's been pregnant, Mom has had one every day with extra onions.

"Hi, Naomi, hi, Mya," says Starr.

"Hey, Naomi, hey, Mya," says Skye.

I lift my wrist. "Hi. Look what I made last night."

They touch my bracelet and smile. Naomi's eyes light up. "OMG, Mya! That looks like it came out of a jewelry store. Will you make me a red one?"

"Sure." I whisper to the twins. "Mean Connie tried to start a fight with Naomi in the Cave."

We all glare at Connie. I keep waiting for her to get a dragon tattoo on her neck or a snake ring in her eyebrow and look like a real bully. I whisper to Naomi. "Before she got here, we didn't have any bullies. And she's a slick one, because you wouldn't even know she was a bully by looking at her. She doesn't even dress like a bully. She wears really cute clothes."

"Those are the worst kind. She's got bully bacteria. I'm sure of it," says Naomi.

I've never heard of bully bacteria, but it sounds like a real disease. The bell rings and we rush to our seats. Mrs. Davis closes the door, and the intercom squeaks to life. "Good morning, It's a beautiful day here at Young Elementary School! Yes, yes, yes it is! Now, let's all stand for the Pledge of Allegiance."

Mr. Winky likes to say our school's initials since they spell Y.E.S.

After the pledge, he continues. "Spirit Week is almost here, so pick up a copy of the Spirit Week schedule from your teacher. This morning you will learn the Spirit Week rules. On a different note, let's congratulate our very own Naomi Jackson, winner of the Junior Miss Lone Star Pageant! We are all so proud of her! Today's cafeteria menu includes fabulous fish sticks, marvelous mashed potatoes, and a beautiful beet salad. This concludes the announcements."

I can't help but smile at Naomi, sitting at her desk, wearing a pretty blue dress that only a princess should wear. Her skin reminds me of the caramel on my Halloween apples, but I think it's her amazing green eyes that made the pageant judges give her the first-place trophy.

Mrs. Davis hands each of us a paper. "Class, let's go over the rules for Spirit Week."

••• SPIRIT WEEK RULES •••

Classroom teachers will award <u>daily points</u> for the following:

5 POINTS *to the Spirit Week partners who: Have the best Spirit Week costumes and/or presentation; and,*

2 POINTS *to Spirit Week "challenge" winners. *Only one challenge per team, per day.*

Acceptable Challenges: You may challenge another set of Spirit Week partners <u>in your class</u> to:

1. *A dance competition: Music will be provided by the competitors. (All dance challenges must take place during recess.)*
2. *Three spelling words or one math question (to be determined by your teacher).*
3. *Cafeteria entertainment: No longer than three minutes.*

1 POINT *to all partners who participate in Spirit Week activities.*

A trade of partners can happen only if all four partners agree. Daily winners will be chosen by the classroom teacher, and scores will be posted in your classroom. The Spirit Week partners with the most points in each grade will receive VIP tickets for the Fall Festival.

The classroom is deep-sleep quiet as we read the rules. Mrs. Davis walks as she talks. "Any questions?"

Silence.

"Then let's open our English books and pick up where we left off yesterday on preparing clear and focused essays with formal introductions, supporting evidence, and conclusions."

I glance over my left shoulder at Naomi. She's the best formal introduction I've made in a long time. She smiles at me and opens her English book.

The morning drags on, but soon it's time to line up for lunch. Naomi's always first, and she lets the twins and me join her. I feel a little strange about cutting in line, so I say thank you to everybody as I *ka-clunk* to the front.

In the cafeteria, Naomi whispers to us. "I'm so excited about Spirit Week. I've been thinking about it a lot over the last few days, and just realized a VIP ticket may help me with something special I'm working on. Let's meet at Mya's house after school, and I'll tell you all about it. Then we can make a plan."

"I'll be there," says Starr.

"I am so there," says Skye.

My heart runs, flips, and jumps all over my insides. "You're coming to my house? After school? Today? You've never been to my house before!"

Naomi smiles. "Is that okay? I mean, that's what best friends do, right?"

I grin and nod. "Yep, that's what best friends do."

"Will Nugget be there?" she asks.

I shrug. "If he is, I'll make him leave so we can talk."

She giggles. "He doesn't bother me."

Firecrackers! I've got so many things to do to make sure everything is double-Dutch perfect when she comes over. I'm going to make Naomi's visit one she'll never forget.

Chapter Four

Ding-dong.

"Nugget, they're here! Hurry up with those smoothies!" I open the door.

Naomi and the twins look down at the long red bathroom rug I put in the hall.

"Why is that there?" asks Naomi.

I grin. "Movie stars and beauty queens are supposed to walk on a red carpet."

Naomi hugs me. "That is so sweet."

I lead them to the backyard. "Nugget's helping me in the kitchen. My mom's napping. She's going to have a baby soon, so she sleeps a lot. I'll be out in a minute with snacks."

I tiptoe to Mom's room and peek inside. She's snoring with earplugs in. Perfect!

I take the tray of veggies while Nugget pours smoothies into plastic cups. Naomi opens the door for us and smiles. "Hi, Nugget. Those look delicious. Did you make them?"

"I most certainly did," he says with his chest puffed out.

She takes a seat and plays with her hair. He rolls his eyes.

"Thanks for the smoothies, Nugget. You can go now," I say.

He salutes and then goes back inside.

I grab a carrot. "Let's play Princess in the Parade. Naomi, you sit on Buttercup. The twins and I will pretend we're watching a parade. You wave at us, and we'll wave back!"

Naomi shrugs. "Okay, but then we have to talk about Spirit Week."

The twins and I help her to climb on top of our mechanical bull. She points at her purse. "Mya, would you get my phone and take a picture of me in case I ever need a rodeo picture for my portfolio?"

I hold the phone steady as she poses. *Click*. Then I skip back to the twins.

"Oh look! Here comes Junior Miss Lone Star!"
I say.

Naomi waves and blows kisses at us. "I wish this bull moved like one in a real parade!"

I half run, half skip back to her. "You want him to move? Buttercup can move! Hold on to that copper handlebar on the back of his neck."

I push the button behind Buttercup's ear just like Dad does when he lets me ride. A woman's soft voice speaks from inside the bull.

"Level One: Easy. Good Luck."

Nugget yells from the kitchen window. "Mya, you're not supposed to—"

I interrupt him. "I know what I'm doing! Giddy-up, Buttercup!"

The mechanical bull gently springs to life, moving up and down like a carousel ride.

Naomi taps Buttercup's neck. "That's enough. I don't like this."

I push Buttercup's button and wait for him to stop.

But he doesn't. I push it again, but he keeps going.

"Mya, I said I'm ready to get off. It's scaring me!" yells Naomi.

I jab my thumb on the button and hold it there.

That should do it.

Oh no. Buttercup's eyes light up. Air shoots through his nose. Good gravy in the navy!

He's alive!

"MOOOOOO . . ."

The woman's soft voice inside Buttercup turns loud and country. "Level Ten: Turbo! Yahoo!"

"AAAHHH!!!"

Buttercup twists and turns ten times faster than he did before. Naomi's flopping around like she's made of Jell-O. "Somebody help me!"

I look for other buttons on Buttercup. "Don't worry, I'll save you!"

My heart pounds so hard I can feel it in my boots. I turn to the twins for help. They're hiding underneath the picnic table with their smoothies and the veggie tray, eating and watching.

Nugget runs toward me. "I'll lift you. Hit the button two times! He'll stop!"

My brother lifts me in the air. "Hold on, Naomi! This is going to be tricky," I say.

When Buttercup's head comes down, Nugget yells. "Now, Mya, now!"

I wrap both arms around the bull's neck like a human lasso. Buttercup takes me up and down. For a moment, I forget about Naomi because this is the best ride I've had all year.

I kick my legs in the air. "Yippeeeeee! Wooo-hooo!"

"Mya! I can't hold on much longer!" Naomi yells.

I press the button twice. Buttercup slows to a stop. Naomi slides down his neck and tumbles onto the grass. The strawberry smoothie is splattered all over the front of her blue dress.

Naomi pouts. "It's ruined, and I just got this two days ago."

What have I done? My shoulders droop. "I just . . . you know . . . I'm so . . . I'll get a towel."

Nugget follows me. "Don't dirty up a towel. It's my week to do laundry," he whispers.

I follow him to the garage. There's no *ka-clunk* in my walk. There's no yippee in my ki-yay. He picks up the leaf blower. "This should do it."

I smile and give Nugget a high five. "Great idea!"

He holds the blower steady and dries her dress. "I'll make you another smoothie."

Naomi has a red stain, bigger than my head, on the front of her dress, and the closer she gets to us, the sadder she looks.

"I'm so sorry," I say, sitting with the twins.

She walks toward the picnic table with her head high, just like a beauty pageant winner. "Don't worry about it, Mya." Very quietly, Naomi sits across from me and folds her arms to hide the stain on her dress. "But it's time to stop playing around. I need to tell you why I have to win those VIP tickets. La'Nique Sydney is coming to the Fall Festival. She stars in *Junior High Spy*. Ever watch it?"

"I watch *Junior High Spy* every day," says Skye.

Starr agrees, "Every day."

"I've seen that show a thousand times. I love La'Nique Sydney," I say.

Naomi grins. "Don't tell anybody, but I just scored a tryout for a part in the show."

My eyes widen. "No way!"

Skye puts her hands to her face. "Are you serious?"

Starr puts her hands on her hips. "You can't be serious."

Naomi nods. "I'm serious. And I just found out that La'Nique is one of the judges for the Battle of the Bands. I have to win those VIP tickets so I can go backstage and meet her. Maybe she'll put a good word in for me before my tryout."

Starr nods. "That's a really good reason to want the VIP tickets."

"A really good reason. We'll help you and Mya win," says Skye.

"We don't really care about VIP tickets. We just want to be there," says Starr.

Naomi leans toward the twins. "You two are amazing friends. Okay, here's the plan. I have to have Mya as my partner even if we have to trade for it. Skye, Starr, make sure the two of you are partners. Then the four of us will do whatever we have to do so that Mya and I have the best costumes and decorations. Let's pinkie-promise."

I link my pinkie to hers. "Promise," I say.

Starr and Skye pinkie-promise, too. Then we all make a toast with our smoothies. After my friends leave, I knock on Nugget's bedroom door.

He sighs. "We're out of bananas and yogurt. No more smoothies."

I lean against the wall. "Everybody's gone."

"Then what do you want?" he asks.

I gently push him. He smiles, gently pushes me back, and then closes his door.

Chapter Five

It's Spirit Week partner-picking day! I'm excited, but Nugget's gripping his backpack straps, staring at the sidewalk, and mumbling. I can tell he has something heavy on his mind.

"Hey, wait up!" Fish holds the straps of his backpack as he runs.

I pat my brother's shoulder. "Here he comes. You better tell him about your plans."

"Hiya, Mya Papaya! Happy Hamburger Day!" says Fish.

"Happy Hamburger Day," I say.

"Hey, Nugget, do you know where the first

hamburgers were made?" asks Fish.

Nugget faces him. "Yes, I do. But Solo thinks the weird holiday calendar is silly."

I roll my eyes. "Who cares what Solo thinks?"

"Solo's a show-off. Somebody needs to let him know that he's not all that," says Fish.

Nugget frowns at both of us, then snaps at Fish. "You're just mad because he's boo-yang cool. He's so cool that I hope he's my Spirit Week partner."

I stop and frown. Fish stops and looks confused. We glare at Nugget, but he won't look at us. I'm so mad that I don't hear the footsteps behind me.

"WATCH OUT!"

My feet leave the sidewalk, and I crash into a pile of leaves. As I spit dirt and pull leaves out of my hair, all I can see is a pair of long legs and black ankle boots beside me. Yikes!

Mean Connie Tate gets up first. I stay on the ground, thinking it might be smarter to play dead. She's wearing an apron with globs of red and blue stains all over it. I bet it's blood and guts from eating a first grader. Even worse, there's an oily blue spot on my favorite brown vest. I wipe at it, but that only makes the spot bigger. A thunderstorm rumbles in my belly. Even though Mean Connie is way taller than me, I get up, stand on my tiptoes, and let her have it.

"You ruined my favorite vest! Why don't you watch where *you're* going? Now I have to spend the whole day at school with . . ."

I look at my brother, then back at the biggest bully in Bluebonnet.

"Was I talking out loud?"

She frowns. "Yes."

Good gravy in the navy.

Mean Connie Tate is going to rip my lips off! She glares at me and points at the stain on my vest. "I won't forget that," she says, and then runs toward school.

Nugget wipes at my vest. "Are you okay? You must have lost your mind yakking back at Mean Connie Tate like that."

Now that she's gone, I stand tall, straighten my vest, and talk like I'm fearless. "Sometimes you've got to speak up for yourself, right, Fish? Fish?"

He's gone.

I pinch my brother as hard as I can. "Today, you're the biggest jerk in Bluebonnet, and I'm glad you're not walking all the way to school with me." I run the rest of the way and wipe at the stain on my vest. My friends are waiting for me as I open the school door.

Naomi's nose wrinkles as she stares at my vest.

"Ew! What's that?" she asks.

"Mean Connie spilled paint on me. She didn't even say sorry."

"It's doesn't look that bad," says Skye.

"Not that bad at all," says Starr.

"She is such a bully," says Naomi.

Students clear the middle of the hall as the four of us walk to class. Just as we get to our classroom door, we stop and stare at Mrs. Davis's desk, where two tall black hats and a stack of papers have all of our attention.

"There they are, the partner-picking hats," I say.

"And I bet that stack of papers next to the hats is the Spirit Week schedules," says Skye.

Starr nods. "Got to be the schedules."

We each grab a copy of the schedule as we pass Mrs. Davis's desk.

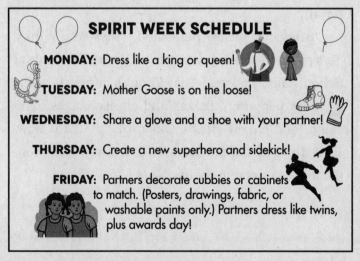

SPIRIT WEEK SCHEDULE

MONDAY: Dress like a king or queen!

TUESDAY: Mother Goose is on the loose!

WEDNESDAY: Share a glove and a shoe with your partner!

THURSDAY: Create a new superhero and sidekick!

FRIDAY: Partners decorate cubbies or cabinets to match. (Posters, drawings, fabric, or washable paints only.) Partners dress like twins, plus awards day!

When the bell rings, Mrs. Davis closes the door.

"Good morning, class! Let's be quiet and wait for the announcements."

The intercom squeaks and we all wait for Mr. Winky's voice.

"Good morning and happy Friday! Before we get started, let's stand for the Pledge of Allegiance."

I try to look at the flag, but my eyes stay fixed on all the Spirit Week partner stuff on Mrs. Davis's desk. "I pledge allegiance to the hats—I mean the flag . . ." Good gravy. Did I say that out loud? Big-eared Michael Silsbee looks over his shoulder and frowns. I pretend I don't see him. " . . . of the United States of America. And to the Republic for which it stands . . ." As I hold my right hand over my heart, I make another promise to do everything I can to win those VIP tickets. " . . . with liberty and justice for all."

"Students, please be seated," says Mr. Winky. "It's partner-picking day here at Young Elementary School! Yes, yes, yes, it is! Today's cafeteria menu includes pepperoni pizzas and cheese pizzas, fruit salad, and carrot sticks. Okay, that's all for now! Have fun picking partners! Yes, yes, yes! This concludes the announcements."

Mrs. Davis stands at the front of the room. "Okay, it's time to get started! Good luck!"

"Me and my partner are going to win those VIP tickets!" says David Abrahms.

"No way! Me and *my* partner are going to win them," I say.

We have a stare-down. Suddenly he smiles. I smile back. I guess that means good luck.

Mrs. Davis holds up two fingers again. "We're going to split into two groups. There will be a group of 'ones' and a group of 'twos.'" She points at David, who sits in the first seat by the door. "Starting with David, he will be a one. Susan, behind him, is a two, the next student is a one, and so on, understand?"

"Yes, Mrs. Davis."

Our room is full of excitement as we count off down the rows. "One! Two! One!" It's time for my row. Michael Silsbee is a one. "Two," I say.

Once we're finished, Mrs. Davis gives more instructions. "I want all the 'twos' to stand in front of my desk. Ones stay seated and write your name on the piece of paper I put on your desk. Then, fold your paper twice, and place it inside a hat when I walk down your aisle; boys in the boy hat, girls in the girl hat."

Once Mrs. Davis collects the names, she walks to the front and stands in front of Susan Acorn. "The girls will pick first."

Susan reaches inside the hat and pulls out a piece of paper. "I pulled Starr Falling."

Starr smiles, but I know she's going to ask for a trade so she can partner with her sister.

Lisa "Lotta-Germs" McKinley is next. She reaches inside the hat. "Yay! My partner is Naomi Jackson!" Lisa hurries to Naomi's desk. "We're partners, Naomi—*achoo*—sorry!"

Naomi wipes Lisa's germs off her. "Yuck! She didn't cover her mouth!"

Mrs. Davis hands Naomi a wet wipe. "Lisa, try to be faster with the tissue."

"Sorry, Naomi," says Lisa.

"Your turn, Mya," says Mrs. Davis.

I pick a piece of paper out of the hat. I'm so excited that I can barely unfold it.

Good gravy in the navy.

The longer I stare at the letters written in green ink on that little piece of paper, the bigger her name gets. My voice flat-out refuses to say what my eyes already know.

"Mya, who is your Spirit Week partner?" asks Mrs. Davis.

I try to tell her. "It's . . . I pulled . . ."

Skye grabs my arm and reads the paper, then bursts out laughing.

"Mya got Mean Connie Tate!"

Some of my classmates cover their mouths in horror. Others laugh. Whispers are everywhere. Mrs. Davis holds up two fingers and everything stops. She grabs the office pad from her desk. "Skye, go to Principal Winky's office right now!"

Skye's crying, "What did I do? I just said Mya pulled Mean Connie Tate."

Starr's crying, too. "That's all she said, Mrs. Davis."

Mrs. Davis rips the paper from her pad. "Tell that to Mr. Winky."

We watch in silence as Skye leaves the room, and Starr puts her head down on her desk.

Naomi raises her hand. "My partner, Lisa McKinley, wants to trade."

"No I don't," says Lisa.

There is something goose-bumpy about Naomi's voice as she tells Lotta-Germs, "Yes, you do want to trade. I really, really, want you to trade, Lisa."

Lisa takes a tissue from her backpack and blows her nose. "Okay."

I have never asked for a Spirit Week partner

trade. I've always kept the person I picked or stayed with the person who picked me. But today, I'm trying something new. I raise my hand and wave it with excitement. "I'd like to trade, too, Mrs. Davis."

Three words come out of Mean Connie's mouth and splat across my face worse than the blue paint she spilled on my vest.

"I'm not trading."

What do M&Ms and Spirit Week have in common?

They both make friends!

Chapter Six

My knees wobble, the room's spinning, and my brain's asleep. I'm going to faint. My best friend locks her two pinkie fingers together. I know what she's telling me, so I give Mean Connie my best stink eye and tell her the same thing Naomi told Lisa Lotta-Germs.

"Yes, you do want to trade. I really, really want you to trade, Connie."

Connie frowns and steps toward me. "Don't tell me what to do, Tibbs."

I step back. "Okay, I'm sorry. You win."

Naomi yells at me. "What are you doing? Don't punk out! Make her trade, Mya!"

Mean Connie's face is hot-sauce red. "She can't *make* me do anything."

Mrs. Davis lifts her office pad from her desk and slowly walks toward my best friend. "Naomi, we don't talk to each other like that in this class. This is your only warning."

I wipe sweat from my forehead. My jaws won't unlock for me to talk. My words must be afraid of Connie, too. Naomi's frowning. Connie's frowning. I don't know what to do.

"Connie, Mya, in the hall, right now," says Mrs. Davis.

Ka-clunk, ka-clunk, ka-clunk.

When we step into the hall, Mean Connie's right beside me, huffing and puffing like Buttercup. There's no doubt in my mind that I'm going to pee on myself. She gets close enough for me to smell bacon on her breath. I stare at the Spirit Week poster on the wall. There's a question at the top of the poster: *What do M&Ms and Spirit Week have in common? They both make friends!*

The red and green M&Ms hold hands in the front of the poster with lots of other M&Ms holding hands behind them. I cut my eyes to Mean Connie. We're definitely not M&Ms.

She faces me. "I'm not trading, and you better not double-cross me, Tibbs."

I haven't forgotten about this morning. She could still rip my lips off and stick them on the wall. The door opens and Mrs. Davis joins us with her hands on her hips.

"Would one of you like to explain what's going on? Is there something I need to know?"

Silence.

Mrs. Davis sighs. "Well, since neither one of you can give me a good reason why I should pair you with someone else, your Spirit Week partnership stands."

"No, wait! I've got a reason. It's . . . she . . ." I'm squeezing my eyes closed, hoping my brain wakes up and helps me out. I open my eyes and point at my vest.

"Take a good look at this, Mrs. Davis! Connie Tate got paint on my vest, and I'm scared she's going to pull my lips off."

Mean Connie turns to Mrs. Davis. "It was an accident. And I never said I'd pull her lips off, even though that's not a bad idea right now."

"Automatic suspension if you put one hand on Mya, understand? Spirit Week is about making friends, not enemies," says Mrs. Davis.

Mean Connie slaps the wall. "I told you I didn't say that! Why won't anybody believe me! I hate this school! It's *worse* than private school!"

"One more outburst like that and I'll write you a pass to Mr. Winky's office."

Mean Connie folds her arms over her chest and stares at the floor. Mrs. Davis wipes at the spot on my vest as if her fingers have detergent on them.

"Mya, this stain should come out in the washing machine. Now, listen very closely to what I'm about to say. Both of you are wonderful girls. Spirit Week is the perfect opportunity for you to get to know each other. Sometimes friendship is like two people lost in the woods. You have to work your way through it together. Success depends on how much time and effort you put into it. Lucky for you, you've got a whole Spirit Week to become friends."

I nod, even though Mean Connie and I would need a Spirit *Year* to figure this out.

Mrs. Davis continues. "I'm going to allow the two of you to stay in the hall, calm down, and face the fact that you *are* Spirit Week partners. If I look out here and see you arguing, or worse, *hear* you arguing, our next walk will be to Mr. Winky's office. Connie, you have promises to keep to me and Mr. Winky, remember? If you lose your partner, then you will have broken your promise. I see this as an opportunity for you and Mya."

I don't want to hear about opportunities. I need a good plan to get rid of Mean Connie. Skye strolls down the hall with a pass in her hand. She gives it to Mrs. Davis as she stares at Mean Connie, then me.

"I'll be back in just a minute. Have a seat, Skye," says Mrs. Davis.

Once Skye closes the door, Mrs. Davis looks back to us. "Girls, I'm waiting on an answer. Are you working together or not?"

Mean Connie stomps her foot and mumbles something only Micheal Silsbee could hear. With both hands she covers her face, but when she removes them, she looks calmer. "Okay, Mrs. Davis, we'll make it work, won't we, Tibbs?"

I'm wondering how Mean Connie changed so quickly from hot-sauce mad to ice-cream happy. I frown at her. "What kind of Spirit Week promise did you make? To stay out of jail?"

Great. My brain finally wakes up and that's what it gives me? Mrs. Davis pats her pockets. I think she's looking for her office pad. I immediately try to make things right.

"I don't know why I said that. I didn't mean it, Connie. Sorry."

Mrs. Davis puts her hands on our shoulders. "Work it out, ladies, and then come back into the classroom and join the rest of us. See you in a few minutes."

I'm alone again with the biggest bully in school, and no witnesses. I'm wondering if I'll make it back to class or if Mean Connie will pull off my lips and stick them to the wall.

She points her finger at me. "I only want to be your partner because I don't want Lisa Lotta-Germs sneezing all over me, and I hate Naomi Jackson."

What the what? Is she telling me that she didn't even want to be my partner? Am I standing out here with someone who doesn't even care about winning the VIP tickets? At first I was scared, but now I'm ready to buck Connie like Buttercup on level ten turbo.

"Well, I didn't want to be your partner at all! You're not only a bully, you ruin people's clothes!

What about that paint on my vest? Who do you think you are? Picasso? And what are you doing with paint at school anyway? We don't have art class," I say.

I've never seen this look on Mean Connie's face. I close my eyes and tuck my lips inside my mouth again. It's quiet. I open one eye to make sure Connie's still there.

"What do you know about Picasso?" she asks.

"I'm not stupid, Connie. Who's never heard of Picasso?"

"I thought you were this dorky cowgirl, running off at the mouth like Annie Oakley."

My eyelids flip open. "What do you know about Annie Oakley?"

She mocks me. "I'm not stupid, Tibbs. Ever been to the Cowgirl Hall of Fame?"

Holy ravioli.

We're eyeball to eyeball, tight-lipped and frozen, in the biggest standoff ever because I'm thinking we both just surprised each other in a very strange way.

She points her long skinny finger at me. "I want those VIP tickets."

I point my short skinny finger back at her. "So do I."

"Pinkie swear," says Connie.

"No way. I already pinkie-swore with Naomi and—"

Connie interrupts me. "I don't care. Naomi Jackson is phony and full of baloney. Listen up, Tibbs. Spirit Week partners are supposed to be friends for the whole week. We need to fool Mrs. Davis into believing we are or she might not give us the points we need to win those tickets. So, next week, we're fake friends. And you better not double-cross me, got it?"

"Got it. We're fake friends. No double-crossing," I say.

Inside Mrs. Davis's classroom, I *ka-clunk* as fast as I can across the room. Mrs. Davis wrote the names of the partners on the board, but I'm only concerned about four of them:

Naomi Jackson—Lisa McKinley
Skye Falling—Susan Acorn
Starr Falling—Mary Frances Whitaker
Mya Tibbs—Connie Tate

I guess since Skye had to go to the principal's office, she didn't get the chance to ask for a trade or even pick her own partner. This is the worst partner picking in the history of Spirit Week. There's a note on my desk. I wait until Mrs. Davis is on the other side of the room before reading it:

Mya
Meet me in the restroom before lunch.
                                    Naomi

I look over my shoulder at my best friend and give her a thumbs-up. We have to fix this problem right away. Hopefully Naomi has a good plan, because we're going to need it.

Chapter Seven

Every day, Mrs. Davis gives us five minutes before lunch to go to the restroom and wash our hands, or we can use the hand sanitizer she has on her desk. I stuff the Spirit Week schedule inside my boot and then rush to the restroom. It's crowded with girls talking and washing hands, and all five stall doors are closed. Skye and Starr stand with Naomi, handing her tissues while she cries.

I step between the twins and hug her. "Of all the names in the black hat, I pulled Mean Connie Tate's. Talk about bad luck. I didn't know what to do, because—"

Naomi pushes me away. She sniffles, but there are no more tears falling down her face as she frowns at me. "Did you forget your promise?"

"Of course I didn't," I say. "Why did you push my hand away?"

Starr frowns at Naomi and then takes my hand. "What happened when you were in the hall with Mean Connie? Are you okay? I was worried about you."

"So worried. And I'm sorry for laughing at you, Mya," says Skye.

"Very sorry," says Starr.

Naomi frowns at the twins. "Why do you care if she's okay or not? She broke a pinkie promise that all four of us made. She didn't just go back on a promise to me. She went back on a promise to you, too! And now our plan is completely ruined. Is this the first time that you haven't been Spirit Week partners with each other?"

They both nod.

"You can thank Mya for that," says Naomi, frowning.

"Hey! It wasn't my fault. Skye laughed and got in trouble," I say.

Starr lets go of my hand. The twins face each other. With no talking, their facial expressions change from plain to pouty. Then they cross their arms at the same time and frown.

"Now what are we going to do?" asks Skye.

"Yeah, Mya, you ruined everything!" says Starr.

Talking in the restroom dies. Stall doors open, faucets stop running. Everyone's staring at me. Chewing my bottom lip isn't helping, but maybe a taradiddle might get everyone laughing, and then everything will be okay.

"I guess I was a little wimpy, but what did you expect me to do—jump on Mean Connie's back and beat her down until she changed her mind? You know, one time when I was riding down the Ohio River on the back of a crocodile—"

Naomi lets out a loud sigh and then interrupts me. "Mya Tibbs broke a pinkie promise."

Mouths open, eyes widen, heads shake. The crowd moves closer to me like bad guys circling the wagons in an old Western movie. This isn't a game.

This is an ambush.

My heart thumps harder. "She's so much bigger than I am. I got scared." I look around the restroom. "Who in here—besides Naomi—is not afraid of Mean Connie Tate?"

Before anyone can answer, Naomi blurts out, "It doesn't matter, Mya. You ruined everything. I thought you were my best friend."

"I *am* your best friend, but I was scared, Naomi!"

She interrupts me again. "I should have known you couldn't keep a pinkie promise. You lie all the time with those taragiggle stories you're always telling."

"They're called taradiddles, and they're made-up stories, you know, just for fun."

A tear falls from Naomi's eye. "You knew how important this was to me, Mya. I can't believe you didn't even try."

Skye gets another tissue. Starr puts an arm around Naomi as she speaks loud enough for every-one to hear. "Does breaking a promise to your best friend sound like fun to anybody in here? Not just a plain old promise. Mya Tibbs broke a very impor-tant *pinkie* promise to me and the twins. Would you stay best friends with someone who did that to you?"

"No," says a girl near the hand driers.

"Nope," says another girl at the sink.

"No way," says Starr.

Why would Starr say that? We've been friends since first grade.

Naomi and I are face-to-face. "Neither would I. Mya, we are no longer best friends."

I back away. What's happening? She didn't say what I *think* she just said, did she? Skye's eyes widen. "What? Wait a minute, Naomi. Don't you think that's a bit—"

Naomi glares at Skye. "I'm not finished talking."

Skye steps closer to her sister. "Why did you say 'no way'?"

Starr shrugs. "I won't stay best friends with a person who broke a pinkie promise to me."

Skye stomps her foot. "But it's Mya!"

I take a step toward Starr and Naomi. "You wouldn't forgive me, Starr? Naomi, I said I was sorry. What else can I do?"

Naomi's voice soars above everyone's as she points at me. "You are a liar, a storyteller, and a no-good fibber. Mya Tibbs fibs. That's what everybody will call you from now on. Good luck with Mean Connie Tate. She'll probably make you mean, too."

Tears leak out of my eyes, and I can't stop them. "What are you doing? I didn't break the promise on purpose!"

Girls back away from me like I stink. I'm looking for help, from anybody, as girls say that ugly nickname over and over on their way out of the restroom.

"Mya Tibbs Fibs," says Naomi.

"Tibber the Fibber," says Starr.

"Stop calling her that," says Skye to her sister.

Starr takes her sister's hand. "Let's go!"

Skye pulls away from Starr and stares at Naomi, then back at me.

"I'm sorry," I say.

Naomi hollers at Skye. "Are you coming with me or staying with her?"

Starr tugs at Skye again. Skye tugs back, but soon they both leave with Naomi. What just happened? Did I just lose my friends? *No!* There has to be some kind of misunderstanding. I'll talk to Naomi at lunch.

∽

I rush back to class, hoping to talk with Naomi before the break bell rings. She's sitting at her desk with Starr standing by her. Skye's not with them. She's sitting at her desk and smiles when I walk in. I stop at Naomi's desk.

"Let's talk about it at lunch, okay? I don't want you to be mad at me," I say.

Naomi doesn't answer. She stares at me as if I'm someone she doesn't know. I *ka-clunk* back to my desk, trying to figure out what I need to say to her so she won't be so angry with me.

There's a note in my chair. I look around, but no one is looking at me. I unfold the note.

> *Tibbs,*
>
> *We're eating lunch together today so we can talk about the schedule. Meet me by the stage. I sit at the detention table.*
>
> *Connie*

I look over my right shoulder at Mean Connie. She glares at me. There is only one word I have to say to that bully.

Okay.

When it's time for lunch, I walk to the front of the line like I always do. Naomi puts her hand up. "What do you think you're doing? You don't belong up here with us anymore. You belong in the back, behind Lisa Lotta-Germs."

My face warms as I walk past my classmates, staring at the floor, on my way to the back of the line in my new place behind Lisa. Moments later, Lisa turns around.

"*Achoo!* Sorry, Mya. I'm not used to anyone

being behind me. Here's a tissue."

I wipe her sneeze from my nose and cheeks. Normally, I'd go off on Lotta-Germs for sneezing on me, but I know she didn't mean it, and right now I understand how she feels.

"That's okay, Lisa," I say.

This morning, I couldn't wait to get to class. Spirit Week partner day has fun written all over it. But something bad happened, and I'm not sure how to make it right. One thing I know for sure as I stand in the back of the line: I've gone from first to worst.

My eyes meet Naomi's as she points at me and says the one thing that hurts me all the way down to my boots. "There's nothing worse than a promise-breaking cowgirl."

Chapter Eight

Connie gets two pieces of pizza and two milks, and then disappears into the cafeteria crowd. I grab a piece of pepperoni pizza, a piece of cheese pizza, and a bunch of napkins in case Connie decides to shove my lunch up my nose. I spot her at the detention table near the stage.

I'm sure Mean Connie owns that table because she sits there every day. I bet she's even carved her name into the wood with an axe. I'm *ka-clunk*ing that way when I hear Nugget.

"Mya, come here a minute! I need to ask you something."

He puts his arm around Solo and smiles as if he just won the lottery. "Fish picked Solo's name and gave it to me. I gave him Bobby Joe McKinley. His sister, Lisa, is in your class."

I glare at Solo, wearing sunglasses in the cafeteria. Two fifth-grade boys walk by and give him high fives for no reason. Solo leans toward my brother and whispers something. Nugget speed-walks to me and cups his hands over my ear. "Since I've been hanging out with Solo, no one has called me Word Nerd Nugget. And he's teaching me how to hoop!"

"And what are you doing for him?"

Nugget shrugs as his voice drops to a whisper. "Nothing really. I do his math homework. No big deal. It's totally worth it, and math is easy for me."

I roll my eyes. "You won't even help me with *my* math homework," I say, walking away. But my brother taps my shoulder and then folds his arms across his chest like Dad does when he's not happy about something.

"One more thing. Did you default on a pinkie promise?"

I feel a cry coming. "It wasn't Dee's fault, whoever that is. It was my fault."

Nugget rolls his eyes. "No, not Dee's fault. Default. It means go back on something."

"I couldn't help it, Nugget," I say. "I picked Mean Connie for my Spirit Week partner, and I was too scared to ask her for a trade, but nobody believes me."

He pulls me over near the big trash can. "You've put me in an unpleasant predicament, Mya. Solo's calling you Mya Tibbs Fibs, and I'm extremely uncomfortable with that."

I can't take all these big words right now. "Is Solo all you care about?"

He jumps when I slam my tray down on the closest table and walk away.

Nugget yells to me. "Mya, wait!"

But I don't. I run out of the cafeteria into the restroom, and lock the door on a stall. I'm no crybaby, but I'm having a hard time making the tears stay away. I reach inside my boot and grab the Spirit Week schedule.

I told Naomi I'd explain everything to her at lunch, and I didn't, and that could cost me another shot at making up with her. I didn't keep my promise to Mean Connie, either. I was supposed to meet her at the detention table. That could cost me my lips.

Spirit Week is over for me before it's even started. I prop both elbows on my legs and hold my face with my hands. Those VIP tickets are history. No free food or first in line for me. Suddenly, the restroom door opens.

"Tibbs, you in here?"

"No."

I pull up my legs, so they can't be seen under the door, and watch a pair of ugly black ankle boots shuffle across the floor.

"I know you're in here, Tibbs. You were supposed to find me, not the other way around. Anyway, I got your pizza."

I put my feet down and open the door. Connie's on the floor with her legs crossed. A plate of pizza sits in her lap. I walk over to the sink, wash my hands, and frown at her.

"I'm not a brat. Everybody thinks I broke my promise on purpose."

"Quit caring about what other people think. Are we going to talk about the Spirit Week schedule in here? This isn't the greatest place to eat pizza," says Mean Connie, looking around.

"I don't feel like talking about the schedule right now, Mea . . . Connie. Sorry."

She grabs the pepperoni pizza, then moves the plate from her lap to the floor, stands, and points her finger at me.

"Listen up, Tibbs. We were supposed to eat lunch together. Then you bailed on me. Now I'm eating pizza on the restroom floor just so we can talk about the schedule, and you're trying to bail on me again. I'm not—"

I interrupt her. "You don't understand. I lost all of my friends today! I've got a nickname that is the ugliest nickname in the whole universe. Everybody in the whole school thinks I'm a promise breaker. Then I pick you for my Spirit Week partner, and you don't even like me! Well, guess what? I don't like you either! If you're going to beat me up, just do it."

She gobbles the last piece of pizza. "I never said I didn't like you. But I never said I did, either. We're Spirit Week partners, whether we like it or not. Even though I don't like to fight, I told Solo and Nugget if they mess with you again, I'd kick their butts and make them lick Lisa Lotta-Germ's tissue bag."

I feel sick at the thought, but it's kind of funny. "Thanks. Solo's not even Nugget's best friend. I don't like him at all. Anyway, I guess we can talk about the schedule at recess."

"I don't do recess," says Connie as she walks to the door. "Don't worry. I'll find you."

I *ka-clunk* out of the restroom, not sure how I feel about having a private conversation with the school bully. She didn't stuff my head in the toilet. She didn't stick my face in the sink and turn the hot water on. And I'm not wearing the pizza she brought in—eating pizza on the restroom floor? That's got to be number one on the gross chart. But I guess bullies eat pizza in restrooms all the time.

I push open the door that leads to recess. Mrs. Davis isn't looking, so I try to blend in by walking around and standing with different groups until I feel like I don't have to anymore. I spot Naomi and the twins practicing cheers over by Nugget, Solo, and a bunch of guys playing basketball. I jog over to them. Skye waves at me, and smiles as she holds Starr's hand.

"Hey, you guys, I think there's been some kind of misunderstanding. Let me explain what happened, okay? I feel really terrible about this, Naomi. I really do want you to meet La'Nique Sidney, and I'll do anything to help you because you're still my best friend."

She frowns. "I can't believe what you did. Me getting Lisa Lotta-Germs as a Spirit Week partner is almost as bad as you getting Mean Connie. It's over. I'm never going to meet La'Nique, and I can forget about winning those tickets. You totally let me down."

I step closer to her. "Don't say that, Naomi. Do you think I care whether or not Mean Connie wins VIP tickets? I'm not helping her win anything! She ruined my vest and *still* hasn't apologized for it. Plus I just watched her eat pizza in the restroom."

"That's just gross," says Skye.

"So gross," says Starr.

I stand in the middle of my three friends. "I'm sticking to *our* plan. Mean Connie is just my Spirit Week partner. You're my friends. We have to figure out how to get Naomi a VIP ticket."

Naomi crosses her arms. "I thought you wanted the tickets, too, Mya Tibbs Fibs."

Mrs. Davis blows her whistle. That's the signal for us to line up.

"I *do* want a VIP ticket, Naomi, but I want you to have one, too. Let's meet at my house again. We can work on another plan."

She doesn't answer me. Instead, Naomi walks toward Mrs. Davis, and the twins follow. I take my place behind Lisa McKinley. After getting stuck with my terrible nickname, I'll never call her Lotta-Germs again.

Back in class, every time I glance Naomi's way, she's looking at me. It's creepy, but I'm sure it's just because she's hurt and angry.

When the after-school bell rings, I *ka-clunk* into the Cave and hear Kenyan Tayler tell David Abrahms, "She broke a promise. Are you going to call her Mya Tibbs Fibs?"

David disagrees. "Over Connie Tate? No way. I would have done the same thing Mya did."

I wait at my cabinet for my best friend. Soon, Naomi, Skye, and Starr pop out of the crowd.

My voice cracks. "I wish you weren't so mad at me."

Naomi frowns. "Don't talk to me. Let's go, girls."

I hold up a hand. "Wait! Your necklace! I brought the beads and string, remember?"

I yank open my cabinet door, and my bag of beads falls to the floor. Hundreds of red beads bounce and roll inside the Cave. Skye moves to help me, but Naomi grabs her arm.

"She didn't help us today. Why should we help her now?"

The twins trail behind Naomi, looking over their shoulder at me. My classmates step over my beads and leave. I'm all alone. Tears roll down my cheeks as I drop to my knees and cover my face so no one will see me cry. Someone touches my shoulder. I turn around, hoping it's Naomi, but it's not. Mean Connie takes the bag of beads out of my hand.

"Take them. I don't care," I say.

She opens the bag. The pockets of her skirt are full of red beads. Carefully, she drops them all back into the bag. When she finishes, she walks toward our classroom.

I yell to her. "Hey, aren't we going to talk about the schedule?"

She sticks her head back inside the Cave. "I'll find you tomorrow. Later, Tibbs."

Yeah, right. There's no school tomorrow, genius. It's Saturday. Geez.

I think back to this morning, when I was so excited about today. I had three friends and a school full of students who treated me like a rock star. Now I'm called Mya Tibbs Fibs, my really nice best friend is super rude to me, and the super-rude school bully is really nice to me.

I stand, and just before I close my cabinet door, I remember something. I didn't tell Mean Connie thanks for picking up my beads. Wait . . . what? Why do I care about saying thank you to a bully?

Everything is wrong. It must be Opposites Day on Fish's weird calendar, and he forgot to tell me.

Chapter Nine

All night Friday, and early Saturday morning, I sit on the floor in my bedroom and listen to sad country music. The songs seem to be written just for me—songs about how my best friend done left me and now I'm all alone, and all my exes live in Texas.

Knock, knock, knock.

"Come on, Mya, it's time to go," says Dad.

I've got my red Tibbs's Farm and Ranch Store shirt on with my jeans and boots. I put my yellow bracelet on again. Maybe it will make me feel better.

After breakfast, we load Buttercup onto the truck. Nugget and I hop into the backseat. I still haven't spoken to my brother since lunch yesterday, and I'm not speaking to him today, either. Dad drives down State Street.

"Nugget, I got a big order for my special corn mix. Go to Storage Barn A, turn on the corn feeder, and fill thirty-five bushel baskets. Be careful; don't waste any."

"Okay, Dad, I'll get it done," says Nugget.

"Mya, I need you to take down all the Bronco Buck Willis stuff and make some kind of rodeo display. Take your time and do a good job. We'll put Buttercup back there, too, so you can create a really nice scene that will make people want to buy things."

"I'll take care of it," I say.

Once we get out of the truck, Nugget, Dad, and I move Buttercup inside and roll him to the back, and then the three of us go in different directions. I walk to the clothing and shoes department, and there he is: a big cardboard cutout of Bronco Buck Willis, Mr. Cancel Britches, Mr. Too Big to Come to Bluebonnet. I should glue his cutout on top of Buttercup and press the Turbo Ride button. But I won't since Dad's trying to get a refund.

Once I get rid of Buck, the only thing I have to work with is Buttercup. I lay a red blanket near Buttercup's front hooves and throw a bag of beef jerky on top of it. That looks so lame. I take a seat on a bench and stare at the bull, but my thoughts are somewhere else. I wonder what Naomi is doing right now. She's probably having fun with the twins. Maybe they're going to the Burger Bar for smoothies.

"Who made this display? A first grader?"

I turn around and swallow all the spit in my mouth when I see Mean Connie Tate standing next to me.

"What are you doing here?" I ask.

She walks around Buttercup. "I said I'd find you. And I did. I went to your house and your very, very pregnant mom said you were here. She's going to download that baby pretty soon, isn't she?"

Connie walks over to the clothing area and grabs a pair of snakeskin boots, a cowboy hat, and a blue bandanna. "I like your bracelet. You make it yourself?"

I take my bracelet off and shove it in the front pocket of my jeans so Connie can't get it.

"Those boots cost over three hundred dollars. That hat is at least fifty. Don't even think about stealing stuff out of our store, Connie Tate. I'll tell my dad!"

She drops everything next to Buttercup and then walks to a different department, collecting weird stuff from all over the store. Now she's got firewood and a skillet from the camping department, hay from the general feed department, a stuffed raccoon, two stuffed rabbits, and two American flags! I can barely see her face because of all the things she's carrying. She comes back over to me.

"You mind if I fix your display?"

I cross my arms. "If you think you can do better, go for it."

She wraps a bandanna around Buttercup's neck and hangs a cowboy hat on his head. The last thing she does to Buttercup is stuff hay in his mouth. I try not to laugh, but I've never seen Buttercup dressed up before.

Soon she stacks the wood like a campfire, places the raccoon and two rabbits near it, and puts the flag and the snakeskin boots near Buttercup. I slowly stand and watch her change my sad, sad display into the best-looking one in the store. There's so much to see, so many colors—I can't believe Mean Connie did this! Customers gather and point at Buttercup and the campfire scene. Dad walks by and a lady grabs his arm.

"Mr. Tibbs, do you have any of those boots for sale like the ones near the bull?"

"Yes, ma'am. Mya, show this kind lady to our boots area."

"Yes, sir."

When I return, he hugs me. "This is spectacular, Mya! What made you think of this?"

I point at Connie. "She did it."

Dad walks over to Connie. "Hi, I'm Mr. Tibbs. Do you go to school with Mya?"

She nods. "Yes, sir. I'm Connie Tate. Johnny Tate's daughter."

Dad chuckles. "Johnny and I went to school together, too! Is he still at the factory?"

Connie nods. "He sure is. Just made operations manager."

"Oh, good for him," says Dad. He reaches into his pocket and gives me ten dollars. "I've got to get back to work. Why don't you and Connie go have a couple of smoothies at the Burger Bar? Maybe your other friends will be there, too! Come back here when you're finished. See you kids later. Good job."

I take the ten bucks and look up at Connie. "You're not thirsty, are you?"

"I'm so thirsty I'm about to die," she says.

"Naomi and the twins are probably there," I say.

She rolls her eyes. "Big wow. Let's go."

Never in all my nine years of life would I imagine walking anywhere with Mean Connie Tate. Yesterday morning, she ran over me like a lawn mower and got paint on my favorite vest. But here I am, walking side by side with her, right to the front door of the Burger Bar.

It's packed with families, kids, and old people. Country music blares from the speakers, and a crowd of people two-step on the dance floor near the salad bar.

"I'm going to grab us a table. Order me a banana-blueberry smoothie with whipped cream, please," says Connie.

Did she just say *please* to me? While standing in line to order, I look around for Naomi and the twins. They're not here. I don't know if I'm happy or sad.

When our smoothies are ready, I take them to the table. Connie takes hers.

"Thanks, Tibbs. That sure was nice of your dad to buy us smoothies."

My mouth is open, trying to find the straw as I stare at Mean Connie. She said please and thank you. Bullies don't say thank you. Mean people don't say please, do they?

"If our dads went to school together, where have you been all of these years?" I ask.

Mean Connie clears her throat. "Private school. I live on Bayou Bend, just three streets down from you. Let's talk about the schedule. Monday is Dress Up Like a King or Queen. Do you have any cool ideas?"

I shrug. "I've got a princess gown somewhere in my closet. I could wear that."

Connie gives me two thumbs down. "Lame. I hear you telling Naomi and the twins those silly taradiddles all the time about wild poker games."

I sit up. "You know what a taradiddle is?"

Connie sighs. "Yes, but think about your poker-game taradiddles. What else has kings and queens?"

I shrug. "Other than a deck of cards, I—"

"Exactly," she says. "Last year, my parents went to a Halloween party dressed like the king and queen of hearts. They won a prize. I think we could win the five points on Monday if we wear those costumes. Yours will probably need some adjusting. You know anyone who can sew?"

I lean back in my chair. "My mom is the best on the planet."

Connie nods. "Good. I'm going to bring you your king of hearts outfit later today or tomorrow. And while we're here, let's talk about Tuesday. You got a problem with Little Bo Peep?"

I glare at her. "Let me guess. For Mother Goose on the Loose Day, you want me to dress like a lost sheep, right?"

She tilts her glass up to get the last drips of smoothie, then puts her cup down. She's got a smoothie mustache above her lip, but I'd never tell her that to her face.

"Yep, I need you to be the lost sheep, okay? I've got an amazing blue gown that's perfect for a Bo Peep costume. If you can nail the sheep's outfit, we might have a shot at winning that day, too! Are you okay with that? You like the idea?"

I want to hold up my fist for her to bump it, but I think about that bully bacteria Naomi was talking about and change my mind. "It's a really cool idea," I say.

I'm not absolutely sure, but I think I just had a good conversation with the baddest bully in Blue-bonnet.

Chapter Ten

Sunday afternoon, Connie drops off the king of hearts costume. I take it to Mom. "Can you make this fit me by tomorrow?"

She holds it up. "Isn't it a bit early for Halloween?"

"Tomorrow's Dress Up Like a King or Queen Day on the Spirit Week schedule," I say.

Mom grins. "Now this is very creative. I'll take it to my magic sewing room. You're going to look so cute! And you should wear your black leggings. Then you'll really look like a walking king of hearts! Wait until Naomi sees you. How's she doing?"

I feel a sad spell coming. "Naomi's fine. I'm going upstairs to find those leggings."

Just as I open my bedroom door, the tears come again. I miss my best friend so much. I know Skye misses me, but Starr is really mad about the Fall Festival tickets. Maybe I'd be mad, too, if I were her. I've got to make them like me again, but how?

I put my boots in the closet and notice last year's boots all slumped over in the corner.

Wait a minute.

Those weren't just regular boots. They were my lucky cowgirl boots, the only pink pair in Bluebonnet with a blue horseshoe burned into both sides at the heels. Mom bought them for me at a garage sale in Fort Worth. I hate knowing somebody else's feet were *ka-clunk*ing around in them before mine. It's hard making up adventures from used boots because they already come with their own boot stories.

But I've got a fix for that. When people ask where I got my bubble-gum-colored two-steppers, I say I won them—in a hard-fought card game—on a horse and kangaroo ranch—in Australia! That sounds so much better than the truth, and it's funnier, too!

Two weeks after I got those boots, I found out they really were lucky! I was in church chewing gum and popped a bubble so loud that it woke everybody up. I knew I was in big trouble, so I rubbed the horse-shoes, hoping they were lucky ones. Dad scooted closer to me, and instead of taking me out of church he asked if I had another piece of gum!

Another time I wore my lucky boots and found a five-dollar bill stuck to a fire hydrant. Right before summer, those boots got so tight that they left marks on my feet. But maybe if I curl my toes, I can still wear them. I sure need some good luck right now, and those boots are a guarantee!

I reach down and rub the blue horseshoes.

If there's any luck still left in you, please help me get my friends back. And if there's any luck still left after that, I'd really like to win those VIP tick-ets.

∾

Early Monday morning, I sit in my pajamas with one hand over my nose and the other in my lap as Mom eats her peanut butter–and–onion sandwich and brushes my hair. "How many braids this morning, Mya?" asks Mom.

"One big fat ponytail, please!"

After she finishes, I rush upstairs and put on the thinnest pair of socks I've got and then tug on my old boots until my feet squeeze into them. I've got the perfect red-and-black bracelets for this outfit, even though the king of hearts probably doesn't wear much jewelry.

As I come downstairs, Nugget laughs at me. He's wearing that dorky crown he got when we went to Burger King on his birthday, four years ago.

"Where's the rest of your king costume?" I ask.

"Solo says dressing up like kings and queens is lame, but I wanted to wear something, so I'm wearing this crown. Our costumes tomorrow are going to be boo-yang good, though."

"You let Solo talk you out of wearing a cool costume? Fish would have never done that. You would have been dressed like King Henry or at least King Kong."

"Leave me alone, Mya. I know what I'm doing."

No he doesn't. I know how much Nugget loves Spirit Week. He and Fish used to plan for days what they would wear.

Mom calls to me. "Come here so I can put makeup on you, Sir King of Hearts!"

I giggle as she makes my eyebrows thicker and gives me a mustache.

"Connie is such a nice girl. I was taking out the trash, and she carried it out for me."

I stay quiet. Mean Connie's got Mom fooled, but not me.

"Done," says Mom. I look in a mirror, and we giggle on our way to the door.

Outside, Connie's standing on the sidewalk, staring at me. "Nice outfit, Tibbs."

Mom waves. "Connie . . . I mean, queen of hearts, you look adorable!"

"Thank you, Mrs. Tibbs," she says.

"Come in for just a minute. I'll put makeup on you, like I put on Mya," says Mom.

"Okay, but remember, the queen doesn't have a mustache," says Connie with a grin.

Mom laughs as Connie follows her inside. She puts lipstick and mascara on the queen of hearts. "Okay, all done," she says.

"How do I look?" asks Connie.

I cross my arms. "You look like that lady on the card."

"Good. Thanks a bunch, Mrs. Tibbs." She strolls to the door. "Let's go before we're late."

We're waiting on the crossing guard to stop traffic for us when Nugget nudges me. "Another meeting. I'm going to the park. See you later," he says.

"Solo's a bozo," I say.

Connie's got a serious look on her face. I think she's about to call Solo something worse than a bozo, but instead, she warns me. "You hate the nickname Mya Tibbs Fibs, but you call other people names? I don't like Solo, either, and your brother shouldn't hang around him, but it's not cool to call people names."

Nugget rolls his eyes. "Like I should listen to a couple of cards. Here comes Fish. I'd like to avoid anything confrontational this morning. I'll see you at lunch," says Nugget.

Fish's hair is dyed black, and most of the curl is gone because it's been combed backward and has a bunch of mousse in it. His costume—a white jacket with white fringe hanging from the arms, and white pants with white shoes—is a big giveaway of who he's supposed to be, but the sunglasses and the guitar strapped to his back make it official.

"It's the king of rock and roll! Your costume is boo-yang awesome, Elvis," I say.

"Thank ya, thank ya very much," says Fish in his best Elvis voice.

Fish, Connie, and I watch Solo throw Nugget a basketball, but he misses it and has to chase it down. Fish waves, and Nugget waves back. I give Fish a little nudge.

"What's on the weird calendar for today?" I ask.

Fish grins. "Happy Toilet Paper Day!" he says.

I nod. "Happy Toilet Paper Day."

"Happy what Day?" asks Connie.

I explain Fish's weird calendar to her, but she just stares at him.

Fish checks out our outfits. "The king and queen of hearts! Very creative."

Connie keeps staring. Fish stares back. I wish someone would say something.

"Well, I'm going to find my Spirit Week partner. See you at lunch," says Fish.

When he's gone, I say to Connie, "He was just trying to be nice."

"I've heard him call me Mean Connie," she says. "I've heard you call me that, too. It doesn't matter, though. All I care about right now are those VIP tickets."

We walk in silence. Those tickets are important to me, too, but I'm trying to help Naomi win, not her. Even though Mean Connie hasn't been scary to me, I still don't trust her. At any moment her bully brain could turn red and she could beat me up so badly that I'd look more like the joker than the king of hearts. Mrs. Davis was wrong about Connie and me. The only friendship I want is my old one with Naomi. And I'm wearing my lucky boots to make sure that happens.

Chapter Eleven

There is a long piece of red carpet leading up to the school door. How perfect. That's what I tried to do for Naomi at my house with my red bathroom rug. Mr. Winky stands by the door, dressed in an Egyptian black-and-gold hat, with lots of eye shadow and mascara. If I didn't know who he was, I'd call the police and scream stranger danger.

"Good morning, King Tut," I say.

"Happy Spirit Week to the king and queen of hearts! Well played, ladies! Well played, indeed! You're going to have a super royal day today at Y.E.S.! Yes, yes, yes you are."

Inside our school, there are kings and queens everywhere, but none of them are dressed like Connie and me. Kids point and laugh at us as we walk down the hall toward our classroom. I don't know if they're laughing at our outfits or if they're laughing because we're partners. Just as I enter the Cave and open my cabinet door, Naomi shows up.

"I got Lisa Lotta-Germs to trade and partner with Mary Frances. So now Starr and I are partners. See how easy that was?" says Naomi.

Connie frowns as she throws her backpack inside her cabinet and then snatches her English, math, and geography books. "Let's go, Tibbs."

I see the twins coming. Even though they're not Spirit Week partners, they're still dressed alike in long, dark-green gowns with tiaras, and holding hands.

"Hold on a minute, Connie," I say.

"Hi, Mya," says Skye.

I give her a big grin. "You look beautiful, Skye."

"Thanks," she says.

Starr's frowning at me. I don't say anything else. Naomi's wearing her Junior Miss Lone Star sash across her gown. She steps closer and looks me over from head to toe. "Those costumes are horrible. And Mya Tibbs Fibs, did you forget that you're a girl? You shouldn't be a king of hearts. You should be a queen of hearts, like her," she says, pointing at Connie.

"Yeah, the queen of hearts," says Starr.

"It doesn't matter," says Skye.

The twins stare at each other. They never disagree. Starr lets go of Skye's hand. Skye frowns at her. Starr rolls her eyes to the left. Skye rolls hers to the right. I've never seen them act like this. Naomi reaches inside her purse and grabs her cell phone.

"Starr, take a picture of me for my portfolio. Mya, where's your brother? Which king is he? Arthur?"

"He's around here somewhere, but he didn't really wear a costume." As I close my cabinet door, I try to make them laugh. "You know, there's only one queen of hearts in a deck, unless you're playing in the backwoods of Alaska, where the bears can't tell the difference between kings and queens. They all taste alike!"

Naomi frowns. The twins look confused.

"Never mind. It was supposed to be a joke," I say.

Connie rolls her eyes, closes her cabinet, and glares at me. "I'm going to the water fountain before the bell rings. You want to go with me?"

Naomi grabs the twins by the hand. "That's where we were going."

I stare at Connie and then run to catch up with my friends.

At the water fountain I'm last in line to get a drink. Naomi finishes and then looks over my shoulder, so I look, too. Solo and Nugget stroll down the hall.

"Hi, Nugget," says Naomi.

He answers in a girlie voice as he tries to walk and wave like Naomi. "Hi, Nugget."

Naomi giggles, takes Skye's and Starr's hands, and walks down the center of the hallway behind my brother, leaving me at the water fountain. Students move to let them by.

"Hi, Naomi, hi, Starr, hi, Skye," they say.

I know what that feels like.

Connie steps around me and gets a drink. She wipes her mouth with the back of her hand. "Let's go, Tibbs. We can't be late."

Instead of strutting like a rock star, I *ka-clunk* toward class with the school bully. No one speaks to me. They just rush past to beat the late bell, and bump my shoulders as if I'm invisible.

Mrs. Davis greets Naomi, Starr, and Skye at the classroom door. "Beautiful outfits, ladies. You look like you just won a pageant."

We stroll in next. Mrs. Davis claps. "The king

and queen of hearts! Very original. Way to use your imagination, girls!"

Even though it's hot and itchy in this card costume, I feel really good about what Connie and I are wearing. She's right. We stand out. We don't look like anybody else, and right now, nobody's calling me Mya Tibbs Fibs. Maybe these lucky boots are working!

The morning goes fast, and soon it's time to line up for lunch. More students laugh at Connie and me. Even after we get our food and take a seat at the detention table, where Connie always sits, boys and girls walk by and laugh. I don't say anything.

A fifth-grade boy comes over and points at my hot dog.

"Are you going to eat that?" he asks.

I shrug. "You can have it—why?"

"Fish challenged Solo to a hot dog–eating contest, and we need more hot dogs."

He snatches the hot dog off my plate and rushes away. Connie and I follow him. There's Fish, stuffing hot dogs in his mouth, with Solo on the other side of the table doing the same as boys and girls root for both guys to eat more. I find Nugget two seats over from Solo. He's not smiling or rooting for either guy.

Mr. Winky blows his whistle. The sound echoes off the cafeteria walls.

TWEEEEEEEEEEEET!

He breaks through the crowd. "What's going on here?"

Fish downs the last hot dog, but his face is now green. My eyes widen as I warn the crowd. "Move back, he's going to—"

Fish bends over toward Mr. Winky.

BLAAAAA-AAAAAH!

Hot-dog chunks splash out of his mouth, milk squirts from his nose, and it all lands on Mr. Winky's King Tut costume and sandals. Every kid in the area says the same thing.

"EEEEEWWWWWW!"

Mr. Winky stares at his feet and then puts his hand on Fish's shoulder. "Elvis, maybe you should go see the nurse."

Fish grabs a napkin and wipes his mouth. "Sorry, Mr. Winky."

I feel bad for him but move away because the smell and the mess make me want to barf, too. Mr. Winky slips and slides as he tiptoes out of the cafeteria. I grab Nugget.

"What happened?" I ask.

Nugget shrugs. "Fish challenged Solo and . . .

I'm very confused right now."

Solo pounds his chest in victory. "I'm the man!"

Fish drags himself out of the cafeteria, holding his belly. He looks back over his shoulder at us. I wave because I don't know what else to do. Poor Fish. I know how he feels.

It hurts to lose your best friend, and when you do, you'll try anything to get him back.

Chapter Twelve

Outside, Mr. Winky shows us some old school moves, holds a clipboard, and watches a dance challenge on the grass. He's with us for recess every day until Friday so the teachers can post the point totals on their Spirit Week boards. Not far away, Naomi shows the twins how to walk like beauty queens. I stand underneath the big oak tree, wishing Naomi would signal me to join them. Watching my friends, knowing that I'm no longer a part of the group, reminds me of the country-and-western song that goes "You done stomped on my heart and mashed that sucker flat." They look like they're having fun. I hope they haven't forgotten about me already.

"Achoo!" Lisa walks up to me, wiping her nose. "Hey, Mya, is it true the reason you wear boots all the time is because you never learned how to tie your shoes?"

Everything on me shakes like a rocket ready for liftoff.

"WHAT!"

Lisa backs away. "I guess it isn't true."

I watch Lisa shuffle back to her friends jumping rope. Two girls walk by me.

"Mya Tibbs Fibs can't keep a promise."

"Mya Tibbs Fibs doesn't know how to tie her shoes!"

I stomp toward the time-out bench and take a seat, because now I just want to be left alone. Who's saying these terrible things about me? I know how to tie my shoes! And it was just one promise! This can't be happening.

After recess, everybody rushes to the Spirit Week board to see who won the big points for today. Mrs. Davis has a special Spirit Week area near her desk. There's a table with stacks of extra Spirit Week schedules, rules, even ideas for anyone to take.

Connie's at her desk, watching all of us come

back from recess. Our eyes meet, but I can't tell if she's happy or sad. So I go and check the board for myself.

MONDAY
COSTUME—5 POINTS
Connie Tate and Mya Tibbs
CHALLENGE POINTS
DANCE—2 POINTS
David Abrahms and Johnny Collins
MATH CHALLENGE—2 POINTS
Skye Falling and Susan Acorn
CAFETERIA ENTERTAINMENT—2 POINTS
No challenges

Jambalaya! Connie and I got the big points today! It's hard to dance in this king of hearts costume, but I'm doing the robot when Naomi stands beside me and stares at the board.

"I guess you're proud of yourself," she says.

I stop dancing, and my mood quickly changes from happy to sad. She's right. I *am* proud for winning the points, but I know my best friend needed them.

"I'm sorry, Naomi. I know how badly you want to meet La'Nique Sidney. I'd do anything to help you. I just don't know what I can do."

Naomi's shoulders droop as she stares at the Spirit Week board. I can see her eyes moving quickly from left to right. She chews her bottom lip just like I do when I'm thinking about something. Slowly she looks at me. Her face is still sad, but now I'm wondering if she's about to cry. She whispers back. "Mya, you know I won't have a shot at meeting La'Nique Sydney without those VIP tickets. It just doesn't seem fair that you would help the biggest bully in the school win and not me. Maybe you were never my best friend."

"That's not true, Naomi! I'm *still* your best friend, and I'll prove it." I close my eyes and think. How can I prove to her that I'm sorry for what I did? I open my eyes, cup my hands around my mouth, lean toward Naomi's ear, and change everything.

"Tomorrow, Connie and I are going to be Little Bo Peep and the lost sheep. Connie's going to be Bo Peep. She's got a really pretty blue dress she's going to wear. You and Skye need to come up with something better than that if you want to get the five points from Mrs. Davis and stay in the race for those VIP tickets."

Time out. I just broke the biggest Spirit Week partner rule on the planet. What the what was I thinking? Oh no.

I just double-crossed Connie.

She can't find out. I won't tell her. Good gravy, I feel so torn in half—I want Naomi to meet La'Nique Sydney, and I couldn't think of any other way to help her.

But I double-crossed my partner.

I miss my friends so much. I want them to like me again. There was no other way.

Naomi's head tilts to one side. "I thought you wanted the VIP tickets as much as I do."

"I do, but I miss hanging out with you and the twins. You really need to meet La'Nique Sydney. That's more important than me being first in line for a bunch of rides. I just want to be your best friend again."

I'm about to cry for a thousand different reasons. Does Naomi realize what I just did for her? Since she's pretty new to this school, she may not understand that telling Spirit Week partner secrets is the dirtiest, rottenest, most double-crossing thing one partner could do to another. But if she does, then she'll understand that I just did the greatest thing I can ever do for our friendship.

"Maybe now you'll believe me," I say.

A little smile appears on Naomi's face. I smile back—maybe she does understand what I just did, and she's going to change her mind and make me her best friend again. She leans in and talks very softly. "How many terrible things has Mean Connie done to you? Have you learned any secrets about her? Did she threaten you to stay quiet about anything? You can tell me, Mya. It doesn't all have to be *exactly* true."

Now she thinks I'm a blabbermouth, but I'm not going to make stuff up. I close my eyes, trying to think of the times I've been with Connie over the past few days. My mind drifts back to the display she fixed at our store, and drinking smoothies at the Burger Bar.

Naomi's voice turns mean and startles me. "What are you smiling about?"

My eyes open. She's staring at my face, frowning.

"This is serious, Mya," she says.

Before I can answer, she turns and leaves me standing at the Spirit Week board.

On the way back to my seat, I catch a glimpse of Connie. She's smiling and making goofy faces at me. I don't want to laugh, but can't help it as I rush back to my seat. Holy moly. She can never find out what I did.

It's time for history, and I reach inside the basket

under my chair for my book. But as I bend over, it dawns on me why I couldn't tell Naomi any horrible things that Connie did to me.

There was nothing to tell.

Chapter Thirteen

Tuesday morning, I'm eating oatmeal when the doorbell rings.

Ding-dong!

"I'll get it," I yell. When I open the door, Solo's standing there in a gray shirt, gray pants, a gray hat, and sunglasses.

"Yo, I'm looking for Nugget" is all he says.

I roll my eyes and holler toward the stairs. "Nugget!"

He takes the steps two at a time coming down. He's dressed in gray just like Solo.

"Who are you supposed to be?" I ask.

He pulls a pair of sunglasses from his back pocket and puts them on. "I'm one of the three blind mice," he says, strutting to the door.

"What are you and Solo going to do about the third blind mouse?"

Nugget shrugs. "Miracles happen. We'll just say the third one got his sight back. Who cares? I gotta go, Mya. Solo doesn't like to wait. Nice sheep outfit. See you later."

I close the door and make my way to the breakfast table. Dad walks by, gives Mom a kiss, and gets his hat, and just before he grabs the doorknob, he turns to me and stares for a long time. Without moving, he calls out to Mom.

"Honey, call Animal Control. There's a sheep sitting at our breakfast table."

I giggle. "It's my Spirit Week costume," I say.

He tries to sound like a sheep. "That's one baaaaaaad costume, Mya! Have fun. See you this afternoon."

Dad leaves, and then quickly comes back. "There's a Bo Peep–looking person out here waiting for her lost sheep to finish breakfast."

I *ka-clunk* to the door. Connie's in the prettiest long blue gown with a white hat that ties underneath her chin. She's wearing her black ankle boots, but it's okay because I'm wearing my boots, too.

"How do I look?" she asks.

"You look awesome! Where did you get that dress? It looks like a Cinderella gown! And is that a real shepherd's staff?"

Connie grips the long stick and holds it straight. "Yep, it's a genuine shepherd's staff. It belonged to my grandfather. Pretty cool, don't you think? I wore this gown two years ago for a . . . special occasion. I'm surprised it still fits me. Ready?"

"Let me get my backpack."

As Connie and I walk down the sidewalk, cars honk and people wave. Some even shout out at us. "Hey, Bo Peep! Glad you found your sheep!"

We laugh and keep walking. Connie touches the cotton on my nose.

"Your mom did an amazing job on your sheep costume, Tibbs. You were right. She's awesome on the sewing machine."

It makes me feel good to hear someone say something nice about my mom. I glance at Connie and then quickly look away. Never in a thousand years would I expect compliments to come out of her mouth. But she's right. Mom is awesome on the sewing machine. Before she started staying at home to get ready for the baby, she helped Dad at the store by working the cash register, ordering supplies, and helping customers. Now that she's home all the time, she's still awesome at a lot of things like Monopoly, making amazing dinners, and just being a mom.

Connie points at two first graders on the other side of the street, dressed like Jack and Jill.

"Is that the cutest thing you've ever seen? Look, Jack's even carrying a pail!"

Connie keeps pointing out costumes, and some are so funny that we have to stop and laugh.

"Okay, Tibbs, we have to talk about tomorrow. What are we going to do for Share a Glove and a Shoe with Your Partner Day?"

I glance down at her feet. "Are you going to wear those boots tomorrow?"

"Yep, I'm wearing these. I've got gloves, too. Are you wearing *those* boots tomorrow?"

I *ka-clunk* harder. "Yep. These are my lucky boots."

"My foot will never fit in those," she says.

I nod. "Your feet are a lot bigger than mine. I mean, my rain boots are the only ones that might fit your feet."

Connie stops. I stop.

"That's genius, Tibbs," says Connie. "I've got a pair of rain boots. Mine are black with white skulls all over them. They're kind of creepy, but I like them. What's on yours?"

I look down at the floor. "They're blue with red teddy bears and hearts."

She's going to laugh, I just know it. Any minute now, Mean Connie Tate is going to call me the biggest baby in the whole United States.

But she doesn't.

Connie shrugs. "Okay, skulls, teddy bears, and hearts. Let's wear the rubber boots, okay?"

My eyes widen and I can barely talk. "You're going to wear one of my boots? I thought you were going to make fun of me."

"Make fun of you? Why? Skulls, teddy bears, and hearts are so different that it may win us some points tomorrow. I'm pumped!"

She fist-bumps me. We giggle and point out more cute Mother Goose outfits on the way. Mr. Winky stands at the door, dressed like Humpty Dumpty.

"Well, good morning, Bo Peep. I see you have your sheep! I'm just all cracked up about Spirit Week! Mother Goose is on the loose! We've got walking nursery rhymes everywhere! Yes, yes, yes we do! Have fun, girls!"

Connie and I cover our mouths so we don't

explode laughing at Humpty Dumpty. The halls look like pages out of Mother Goose's nursery rhyme book! We play a game of Guess the Character as we walk toward our classroom.

"There's Little Miss Muffet," says Connie.

"And Little Jack Horner," I say.

Fish strolls down the hall with a toy trumpet on a string around his neck. He's wearing a light-blue T-shirt with light-blue shorts.

"Hiya, Mya Papaya! Are you Mary's little lamb, or are you lost, looking for Bo Peep?"

"Well, Little Boy Blue," I say, "I'm with Bo. Where were you this morning?"

He shrugs. "Woke up late. Anyway, happy Oak Day, Mya Papaya."

"Happy Oak Day, Fish," I say.

Connie smiles. "Happy Oak Day, Fish."

He has a whale-size grin on his face. "Thanks, Connie!"

Inside the Cave, Connie leans her shepherd's staff against the wall. Out of the corner of my eye, I see a hand swipe at it.

Clankety-clank!

Naomi and the twins stand behind Connie's shepherd staff lying on the floor. I glance toward

Connie. She's breathing like Buttercup, so I walk over, pick up her staff, and put it back where it was.

Skye touches my arm and I grin at her. She has on a farmer's hat and overalls. Maybe she's Old MacDonald—I'm not sure—but Starr's dressed in the coolest sheep costume I've ever seen.

The whole outfit reminds me of a onesie covered in wool. The hood on her costume has floppy ears on it. I can't believe how her hands and feet look just like hooves in those black socks. Her outfit makes mine look horrible. All I've got is a bunch of cotton balls stuck to my blouse and pants, with cotton on my nose.

"Where did you find that sheep's outfit? It looks so real compared to mine," I say.

"I didn't know sheep wore cowgirl boots," says Starr in an ugly tone. I don't say anything smart back because I'm trying to get Starr and Naomi to be friends with me again. But after a moment, Starr's eyes look away. Maybe she felt bad for being mean.

Naomi's blue gown is gorgeous. It's got silver lace on the collar and at the bottom that matches her silver slippers. The front of her dress has two rows of silver zigzaggy lines that go all the way to the back. Her blue bonnet has silver around the edges, too.

"Wow, Naomi, are you . . . Bo Peep, too?" I ask.

She's still staring at Connie, who's getting books out of her cabinet.

Naomi crosses her arms. "Well, Connie, are you supposed to be Bo Peep?" she asks.

Connie ignores her. Naomi walks slowly to her cabinet, which isn't far from mine, and makes fun of us.

"That is the saddest Bo Peep and lost sheep costume I've ever seen. Mother Goose would be so mad if she saw the two of you. If it comes down to who's the better Bo Peep, I'm going to win. Anyway, Connie, haven't I seen you in that dress before?"

Connie slams her cabinet door and leaves the Cave.

"Wait, Connie! We're supposed to walk in together, remember?"

She doesn't stop. Naomi giggles. As Connie storms off, a part of me hurts because I told Naomi our plans. But the other part of me feels good seeing Naomi happy. I close my cabinet and stand next to her, hoping she'll finally talk to me. And she does.

"Where's Nugget?"

My shoulders droop. "He should be here soon," I say. I hoped she'd tell me that I'd made up for the mistake I made by giving her the tip about Connie and me, but she didn't.

Naomi moves closer to me. "So, Mya, what are you and Connie wearing tomorrow?"

I think about Connie, and how hurt she looked when she walked to class alone. I didn't know Naomi and Starr were going to be copycats. I still want to help Naomi, but I'm not going to give away any more Spirit Week secrets.

So I shrug. "Not much you can do with just sharing gloves and boots."

"Let me know when you find out." She turns to Skye and Starr. "Let's go, girls."

I touch Naomi's shoulder. She frowns, but I say what's on my mind. "I was hoping we could hang out again. I mean, since I'm trying to help you win the tickets."

Naomi lets out a belly full of air. "Not yet, Mya. But I'm thinking about it."

I've got hope running up and down my insides because Naomi didn't give me a flat-out no. My lucky boots are working! Maybe I have a chance to be her best friend again. I rub the horseshoes on my boots and then *ka-clunk* into class. The first face I see is Connie's. I quickly take my seat. Maybe if I don't look at her, I won't feel so bad.

But I feel horrible.

There's got to be a different way to make Naomi

like me again. Maybe if Connie and I win, I'll give Naomi *my* VIP ticket! What a perfect idea! That way, she'll get to meet La'Nique Sydney, and I won't hurt Connie! That will prove to Naomi that I'm still her best friend, and hopefully she will feel the same way about me. I can't believe I'm thinking about giving my VIP ticket away. But Naomi's worth it.

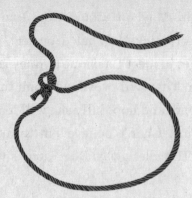

Chapter Fourteen

Today I'm wearing three braids, one on each side of my head, and a big one in the back.

I've got my blue boots on with the teddy bears and hearts. My lucky boots are at home, but maybe nothing bad will happen today. I'm still wondering why Connie didn't make fun of me yesterday when I told her about these rubber boots. I've had them since second grade, and now more than ever they look like boots for babies. Why am I just now noticing that? I stick my gloves in my pocket and follow Nugget outside. He's wearing his batting gloves and his favorite basketball shoes, and yawning and wiping his eyes as if he's trying to wake up.

"Up late last night?" I ask.

"Math is getting harder. I don't know how much longer I'll be able to do this for Solo."

"You shouldn't be doing it at all."

He frowns at me. "Heard anyone call me Word Nerd Nugget lately?"

I stare at the sidewalk as I walk. "No, not really."

He nods. "That's why I do his math. It's our agreement. Solo lets me hang out with him, I get to play basketball on his team, and for that, I do his math homework. It's been relatively easy so far, but now we've moved into working with commutative, associative, and distributive properties, prime numbers, and oh my gosh, the teachers have taken division and multiplication to a totally different level. It's hard stuff, Mya. And Solo is expecting me to get everything right."

"So, what if you told him you couldn't do his math homework anymore?"

"That's not an option. I could get beat up. A deal is a deal," he says.

I wish I had someone to stop kids from calling me Mya Tibbs Fibs, but I don't. And anyway, if I had to do their math, they'd flunk.

I look behind me and spot my Spirit Week partner.

"There's Connie. I'm going to walk with her."

Nugget stands at the corner of State Street. "You know where I'm going. See you later."

When she sees me, Connie slows down. "Very cool," she says.

"Check 'em out. Bull riding gloves with wings!"

Connie holds up one hand. "I've got motorcycle gloves. There's no fingers on them."

She takes my boot, then hands me hers. I'm not sure who laughs first, but Connie's got a bad case of the giggles.

"We look silly," she says.

I look down at my mismatched rubber boots and giggle with her.

"Tomorrow is Superhero and Sidekick Day. You want to meet at my house after school to talk about what we're going to wear? Nugget makes really good smoothies," I say.

Her smile fades. "No, thanks."

"Aw, come on, that's what friends do."

Why the why did I say that?

"Friends are nothing but trouble. You should know that by now," says Connie.

"I meant to say fake friends," I add as we walk.

Connie grins. "Fake friends wearing mismatched rubber boots. Yep, that's what we are. Anyway, can you sing or rap or dance?"

"Of course!" I say. "I can do all of those things, why?"

"I think we should challenge Naomi and Starr to a cafeteria talent contest. We need the extra points, especially if we don't win the five points today."

I stop walking. "I can't challenge Naomi. I want her to be my friend again."

"No you don't," says Connie.

I frown at her. "Naomi Jackson is the best friend I've ever had."

Connie sighs, and steps closer. "Tibbs, what I'm about to tell you might hurt, but it's the truth. Naomi doesn't like you. She likes Nugget."

There's a rumble in my stomach, and it's not because I'm hungry. My skin's hotter than it was a few seconds ago as I ball my fists up.

"Take that back! You're just being mean!"

She blinks so quickly that I wonder if she's going to cry. But instead, her eyebrows scrunch and her nose wrinkles. "Think about it, Tibbs. How many times does Naomi ask you about your brother? I hear her ask all the time. Test her yourself! Tell

Naomi you can get Nugget to like her, and see what she says. She is so fake."

I yell at her. "You're the only fake friend I've got, Mean Connie!"

She backs away from me. "Whatever, Tibbs Fibs."

"Stop calling me that!" I shout.

"I will, when you stop calling me Mean Connie!"

She's eyeballing me. I'm eyeballing her. "Fine!" I say, and walk by her as fast as I can.

I almost liked her. What a megamistake that would have been. I wish I had never picked her name out of the partner hat. It's her fault my best friend is mad at me. The only friend *she's* got is me, and our friendship is fake.

"Tibbs, wait!"

Connie runs to catch up. "Look, I know you don't believe me. I know you like Naomi a lot. But I just don't want you walking around thinking Naomi is a nice person. She's not. I know for a fact."

I grip the straps of my backpack. "You don't know anything about her!"

She stomps her foot. "You're wrong, Tibbs! I know *everything* about her."

Even though Connie's standing right beside me, I know she's really not here. She's daydreaming, lost in space, totally distracted by something. Whatever it is, or wherever she is, it takes all the anger out of her face and replaces it with hurt.

"I went to private school with Naomi for a year. If you ever want to know the truth about her, ask me, or test her yourself. I still want those VIP tickets for the Fall Festival, and I think we need to do a challenge if we want to stay in the race to get them. I'm going to tell Mrs. Davis as soon as I get to class. I'm really sorry if I hurt your feelings. It's just that I wanted you to know the truth before she hurt you like she . . ."

Connie's face wrinkles up, like her stomach hurts. She looks down at the sidewalk and mumbles something before looking back at me. "Anyway, I'll see you in class, Tibbs."

As Connie walks away, my mind goes back to last Friday, when I tried to apologize to Naomi but she wouldn't accept it. In the last four days, I've had fun with Connie, even though she just made me bone-breaking mad, but I don't think she did that on purpose. Seriously, I thought I'd be dead by now, being her partner. But I'm not. Now Connie's trying to apologize, and I'm treating her the same way Naomi treated me.

Most of all, after what I did on Monday, this is

the least I can do to try to make it up to her. Even though she doesn't know, maybe it will make me feel better.

"Hold on," I say, running toward her.

She stops and turns around. I shrug twice before anything comes out of my mouth. "I'm sorry for yelling at you. I won't do that again. And I'm sorry for calling you Mean Connie. I used to believe you were, but I don't anymore. I don't even know why I said it, but that won't happen again, either. We can do the talent challenge. And I'll find out if what you said is true. But if it isn't, you owe me a large smoothie at the Burger Bar." I hold out my fist. "Deal?"

Connie bumps my fist and smiles. "That's a deal . . . Mya."

I look up at her. "You called me Mya! You always call me Tibbs."

Connie shrugs. "People I don't like or care about, I call them by their last names."

I grab the straps of my backpack. "Are you saying you like me?"

Connie smiles. "I'm just saying things may be changing."

I'm not sure how I feel about what Connie just said. It didn't scare me. I'm not mad. And I don't feel sick, but I definitely like how she says *Mya* more than I hate how she says *Tibbs*.

Mr. Winky greets us with a gardening glove on one hand and a lady's white church glove on the other. One of his shoes is the normal black one that he wears with his suits, but his other foot is stuffed in a red high heel. There are black scuff marks all over the side of the red shoe. I bet those came from him losing his balance.

I laugh out loud. Connie covers her mouth, as Mr. Winky greets us. "Howdy, Mya. Good morning, Connie. Happy Share a Glove and a Shoe with Your Partner Day! My secretary's high heel matches my outfit, don't you think? Yes, yes, yes. Sharing is caring and, for me, very daring! Have a wonderful day today!"

As we stroll toward class, two girls walk by us whispering "Mya Tibbs Fibs," "Promise breaker," "Mean Connie Tate," and "Spirit Week partners" loud enough for us to hear. Connie and I keep walking.

The hall is full of *flip-flop/ka-clunk*s, *boomp/flap*s, and *squeak/clink*s from mismatched boots, sandals, and shoes. One boy wears a green basketball shoe and one black cowboy boot. A girl has one foot flip-flopping in a gold sandal, and the other foot *ka-clunk*s in a shiny orange boot. Two girls have switched bedtime slippers. One slipper is a duck and the other is a teddy bear. Everyone looks crazy, but nobody looks as good as Connie and me until I see David Abrahms and Johnny Collins. Students move to let those guys strut down the center of the hall.

Red lights flash from the front, back, and sides of one of their shoes when they take a step. Their other shoe has blue lights flashing. David's snapping his fingers, wearing one red glitter glove and one blue one. Johnny's wearing the same. They even have glittery red and blue hats! David plays music on his cell phone. Everybody's watching as they come down the hall.

Suddenly the crowd splits. Naomi and the twins *click-clack* toward me in mismatched shoes.

"Hi, Mya," says Skye, wearing a bear-claw slipper and a white tie-up boot that stops at her knee, with red and yellow mismatched gloves on her hands. "Your boots are hilarious."

I giggle. "Yours are funny, too. Does Susan Acorn ever get upset that you spend most of your time with Starr and not her? I mean, she *is* your Spirit Week partner."

Skye shakes her head. "Susan understands how close I am to my sister. She's just having fun with

Spirit Week and doesn't care about the VIP tickets, just like me and Starr. We're good."

Starr's *click-clack*ing around in a glass slipper like Cinderella's on one foot, and a pretty blue sandal on the other. Long white gloves cover her arms up to her elbows. Naomi strolls over in gloves and slippers that match Starr's.

"Where's Nugget today?"

I think about what Connie told me. "I don't know. He's around here somewhere."

Naomi doesn't ask anything else, like how I'm doing, or even what Connie and I are working on. Why hasn't she decided to be my best friend again? What's taking her so long?

Once the bell rings, Mrs. Davis closes the door. Connie raises her hand. "Mrs. Davis, Mya and I would like to challenge Naomi and Starr to a cafeteria entertainment challenge today."

Chapter Fifteen

It's so loud in the classroom that Mrs. Davis has to clap her hands to shut us up. Everybody's talking about Connie and me challenging Naomi and Starr. Mrs. Davis holds up two fingers.

Silence.

"Participants must remember to bring their own music, or props if you need them."

I hope lunch gets canceled, or the cafeteria burns down.

But it doesn't.

Time flies by faster than ever. My stomach is full of butterflies as we line up for lunch. Connie stands with me at the back of the line.

"What are you going to do for the challenge, Mya?"

"I guess I'll sing."

"Okay. I'll back you up."

I turn around. "You're going to sing backup?"

"That's not what I meant," says Connie.

In the cafeteria, I spot Nugget sitting with Solo. They're not sharing gloves or shoes. My brother looks my way, and I roll my eyes. Yesterday he was a blind mouse. To me, he's still blind if he thinks Solo is a better Spirit Week partner than Fish.

Connie and I set our trays down at the detention table and eat. Halfway through lunch, Mrs. Davis stands near us with a microphone in her hand.

"Boys and girls, we have a cafeteria entertainment challenge!"

"YAY!"

Mrs. Davis continues. "Connie Tate and Mya Tibbs have challenged Naomi Jackson and Starr Falling. Naomi and Starr, you're up! Please come to the stage."

Naomi and Starr take their time walking toward us. Connie and I move so they can use the steps to climb up on the stage. Suddenly Connie gets up and walks toward the cafeteria door. Where is she going?

When Naomi gets close enough, she whispers to me.

"Why didn't you tell me about the challenge? You knew about it and didn't warn me. I thought you were my friend. Where's your partner? I bet she left you to do the challenge all by yourself."

My food doesn't feel good in my stomach. Mrs. Davis hands Starr the microphone. Naomi takes her cell phone from her purse.

"Mrs. Davis, will you take a picture of me before I get started? I may need a photo of me onstage at school for my portfolio."

"Sure," says Mrs. Davis.

After the picture, Naomi presses a button on her cell. A song from the movie *Annie* comes on. Students stop eating and listen as Naomi sings, and Starr tries to be a ballerina.

"'The sun'll come out tomorrow.'"

I look around the cafeteria for Connie. I don't see her.

"'Bet your bottom dollar that tomorrow there'll be sun!'"

When it's over, everybody claps.

"Yeah!" "Awesome!" "Way to go, Naomi!" "Good job, Starr!"

"Now, the challengers, Connie and Mya," says Mrs. Davis. "Connie, are you in here?"

Where is she? Naomi's right. She bailed on me.

Mrs. Davis has a sad face. "Well, I guess the challenge is—"

"Wait! I'm here! Sorry I'm late," Connie says. "It will only take me a minute to set this up."

The cafeteria buzzes with giggles and whispers of "Mya Tibbs Fibs" and "Mean Connie Tate." Connie rushes to the stage, unfolds her easel, sets a huge writing tablet on it, and then pulls out five crayons.

Good gravy in the navy.

Why is she using just five crayons? I sure hope she has a plan. The laughter is so loud that Mrs. Davis has to put up two fingers. Connie pulls a cell phone from her pocket and starts pushing buttons. "Here, I've got music for you, Mya. What do you want to sing?"

My heart thumps hard. I've got a belly full of butterflies and bumblebees. "I'll sing anything that will make us win," I say.

Mrs. Davis comes onstage. "Ladies, time is running out. You must do something soon."

"Okay, we're almost ready," says Connie.

She points to a song on the screen of her cell. "Do you know this one?"

"No," I say. Connie lets out a loud sigh. "Hurry and think of something, Mya!"

Students giggle and point at us. I'm looking everywhere for a clue of what I could sing. Then I see the recess box with all the equipment inside.

"Mrs. Davis, may I use one of the jump ropes over there?"

She nods. "Sure, go ahead!"

I skedaddle down the steps, grab a jump rope from the box, and hurry back. I tie a good lasso knot on one end and glance back at Connie. She gives me a thumbs-up, so I twirl that rope in the air and sing my song as if I'm on television.

"She'll be ropin' all the cattle when she comes!
Ruby gems and yellow diamonds on her thumbs.
Mya Tibbs is such a winner,
Because winning is what's in 'er.
She'll be ropin' all the cattle when she comes!"

Students put their forks down and begin to clap the rhythm to my song. Some get up, loop arms, and do-si-do. I hold the microphone with one hand and pretend as if I'm roping things with the other! I even try to jump through my lasso, but it gets tangled on my rubber boots. Nobody seems to care! Things are going so good, I sing the second verse and keep twirling!

"She'll be ropin' all the cattle when she comes!
She'll be using all eight fingers and two thumbs.
Mya Tibbs is such a winner,
Because winning is what's in 'er.
She'll be ropin' all the cattle when she comes!"

We're having so much fun with the song that Mrs. Davis has to come onstage and take the microphone away from me. "Time's up! Thank you, Mya. Connie, would you like to show everyone what you were doing while Mya was singing?"

Connie stands, takes the drawing tablet from the easel, and turns it around for all of us to see. My mouth opens. I drop the mike. She drew that with crayons?

Everyone's staring and pointing. "Aaaaaahhh." "Oooooohhh."

There's a sky full of blue diamonds and red rubies and other colorful gems. The sun makes them sparkle over a field full of cows with someone on a horse with a lasso riding up behind them. I'm speechless. Connie drew what I sang. She drew it even better than I sang it.

And she did it with five crayons.

Fish stands up again. "That is boo-yang awesome!" he shouts.

"Yeah! Connie and Mya are the best!" yells Nugget, as the crowd claps and cheers.

Naomi runs onstage and grabs the microphone off the floor. "That's not fair. Mrs. Davis, we didn't actually see Connie draw that picture. Mya and Connie should be disqualified."

The clapping stops. Mrs. Davis takes the microphone from Naomi. "Even though I really don't like the accusation, Naomi, you have a fair point. I'll take it under consideration, and results will be posted in my classroom on the Spirit Week board."

"I drew it just now!" yells Connie as she folds up her easel.

There's a creepy quiet in the cafeteria until Mrs. Davis lifts the microphone again. "Settle down, people! All right, let's just finish eating."

There's no way I can eat. Connie's telling the truth. She didn't know what song I was going to sing until I sang it. Then she drew it.

I walk down the steps and sit at the detention table. I didn't see Connie draw that picture, but my guts tell me she did. She brings her things from the stage and leans them against the wall, then sits down next to me. She's shaking, and I don't think it's because she's cold.

"I drew that picture while you were singing. By

the way, you did an awesome job."

"Thanks, Connie."

As I sip my milk, Connie pushes her tray away, shakes her head, gathers her easel, her backpack, and the rest of her stuff, and leaves the cafeteria. I look over at Naomi. Our eyes meet. Something doesn't feel right. I know Naomi needs the VIP tickets, and I know she needed me to be her partner. But if things had worked out, and I *was* Naomi's partner, I never would have agreed to hurting people.

As I take my tray to the conveyer belt, I get a few thumbs-ups and pats on the back. A fifth-grade girl actually smiles at me. Connie and I may not be the coolest girls in this school, but right now, we are definitely the most popular Spirit Week partners.

I need to make sure Connie's okay. Last week I wouldn't have cared one way or the other, but now I do. I'm not sure where she goes instead of recess. She might get mad at me for spying on her, but that's the chance I'm going to take. So if I'm going to follow her, I'd better leave now while I'm still brave enough to do it.

We love
Sprit Week "Beary"
much!

Chapter Sixteen

While the cafeteria is crowded with students standing and holding trays, I sneak out and take off my rubber boots so they won't make squeaky noises down the hall. I've seen plenty of movies on how to follow people without them knowing it. I stay back as Connie hurries down the kindergarten-through-third-grade hallway. Fourth and fifth graders call it K3 hall.

Wow, look at the awesome Spirit Week posters on these walls! There's one with teddy bears holding hands. *We love Spirit Week "Beary" much* is written underneath. On the other wall, there's a poster with ninjas doing martial art moves with *Spirit Week Is Ninja Cool* in big letters. These posters are just as good as the ones on the fourth- and fifth-grade walls!

Way down at the end of the hall, Connie stops in front of a room. She pulls a key from her pocket and unlocks the door. I wait until a light comes on. That's when I make my move.

I dash down the hall, and then slide across the floor in my socked feet until I reach the last room. I stand with my back against the wall and then lean forward so I can look through the glass in the door, but my boot hits the doorknob as if I knocked.

Busted.

The door flies open. Connie looks bigger than she ever did before. My voice gets scared again and won't come out. I take two deep breaths, letting both of them out slowly.

"Did you come down here just to do breathing exercises? You were spying on me, weren't you? You followed me. I don't like that."

Lucky for me, my voice comes back. "Did you see the Spirit Week posters in K3? They're awesome, aren't they? Anyway, when I was in Washington,

DC, I walked down this dark, empty alley on my way to meet the president. I had some top-secret papers for him, and . . ."

Connie gives me a stink eye that makes my toes curl. "Go away, Mya. I'm not sick, and I'm not lost, and I'm definitely not in the mood for one of your taradiddles."

"Sorry, Connie. I was worried about you. I knew you were upset when you left the cafeteria. I mean, I guess I'd be mad too. And I believe you when you said you drew that picture. It was awesome. Can I come into your hideout? We can talk about what we're going to wear for Superhero and Sidekick Day tomorrow."

She leaves the door open. The words *Utility Room—Employees Only* are written across the glass in the window. I knew it! She's no student.

Connie Tate is the janitor!

I look inside before stepping in. My brain's thinking a thousand different things Connie may be doing back here. The more I think, the faster my heart beats. This must be where she stores her mop, or stolen goods. There's an easel, and a huge drawing pad leaning against a big sink. Wait a minute . . . what is this place? I step inside. My brain relaxes. My heartbeat calms down as my mismatched rubber boots slide out of my hands.

It's . . . it's . . .

Beautiful.

The walls fill my eyes with blues, browns, reds, yellows, oranges, and greens. On one wall, a drawing of the sun sitting between two snowcapped mountains makes me shiver as if I'm up there, freezing in the cold. On a different mountain, lions, goats, and snakes live on the rocks and in the grass, but those huge eagles soaring near the waterfall look so real that I hold out my arm for them to land on it.

"Hands off, Mya."

My eyes widen. "*You* did this?"

She doesn't answer me. Then I notice long pieces of paper; the same paper I've seen on the walls used for the Spirit Week posters. My brain goes crazy as it remembers things like:

Her apron with red and blue paint on it.

The blue paint spilled on my vest.

The display she quickly put together at Dad's store.

The brown paper in this room.

I put my boots on. "*You* made all the Spirit Week posters, didn't you?"

She still doesn't answer, but she doesn't have to. I can tell it in her face as she holds her chalk and wipes something I can't see off the brown drawing paper.

Connie sighs. "Let's talk about our costumes for tomorrow. Then you can leave. I'm really busy."

I don't want to talk about costumes right now. I want to stand here and look at the pictures. On another wall, things are not so easy to figure out. There is a drawing of a bowl of fruit with a big cheeseburger in it. To the left is a woman's head with spaghetti for hair, and a spoon sticking out of her ear.

But then, on a section of that same wall, away from all of the weird drawings, I notice a sketch so awesome that I walk toward it as if it's calling me.

"Who are they? Are they new? I've never seen these princesses before."

Connie puts the chalk down. "They're not princesses waiting for some dorky Prince Charming to come save them. They're warriors who guard and protect the galaxy from harm. I call them the Girl Guardian Court—the GGC."

In the very center of the wall, a warrior rides a horse—but not an ordinary horse. It's huge with a brown coat that has some red in it everywhere except at the bottom of each leg, where a long, snowy-white coat of hair grows out of nowhere. I point and try to say something, but only one thing comes out of my mouth.

"Clydesdale."

Connie stands next to me. "They're the biggest reason why I want the VIP tickets. I want to meet the trainers and maybe get to brush one down or take that awesome trail ride."

"Wow, a secret art room—and it belongs to you. How cool!"

I would have never guessed in a million years that Mean Connie Tate could love something as beautiful as a Clydesdale, or that we would have something like that in common.

She points a piece of chalk at me. "You better not say a word to anyone about my drawing room, understand? You had no right following me. This could ruin everything. Swamp rats like Naomi might crawl in here and trash everything."

I don't like that she called Naomi a swamp rat, but for a moment, I see a different Connie; someone who cares about something. As calm as I can, I walk over to her. "I won't tell a soul. And I really like the guardians in the GGC."

"You swear?"

"Swear," I say.

It's quiet for a moment. Connie picks up a piece of chalk. "You really rocked the cafeteria today."

I smile. "Thanks. Hey, Connie, what does that C.T. stand for on the side of your boots? No wait, let me guess . . . crooked toes . . . cockroach train . . . cowgirl two-step . . . candy Twizzlers . . ."

She slams her chalk on the table. "Connie Tate! The C.T. stands for Connie Tate. You just went from great singer to mosquito brain!"

I laugh. The frown leaves her face and she laughs with me. I shuffle to the door.

"I was just joking. I better get to recess before Mrs. Davis realizes I'm gone. See you later."

The posters in the K3 hall look even better to me now that I know my partner made them. But Connie's made me promise to keep my mouth shut, so I will. She's probably the only person in this whole school who's hated more than me right now. Connie's right. Someone would trash her room, just because it belongs to Mean Connie Tate, the girl who broke her brother's fingers and trashed the bakery.

A thought pushes its way to the front of my brain. I've been Spirit Week partners with Connie Tate since last Friday, and I haven't seen her do anything that would make me think the gossip about her is true. Am I the only person who's ever thought that the rumors might be lies?

Since Friday, Connie has helped my mom, helped me at Dad's store, made me laugh, and said that she was sorry and that she doesn't like Solo. The more I think about Connie Tate, the more I realize that we have lots of things in common.

Chapter Seventeen

I sneak out to recess again, hoping Mr. Winky doesn't spot me. He's judging another dance challenge between two fifth graders, so I make my way toward a crowd of girls jumping rope and playing clapping games and think of what I'm going to say to Naomi. She's been my best friend for almost a whole month, and I want more than anything for Connie to be wrong about her. I'm kicking rocks when I hear Naomi's voice.

"You should have warned me about the challenge."

I shrug. "I didn't know about it until this

morning. But I bet Mrs. Davis won't give us any points after you accused Connie of trying to cheat."

Naomi giggles. "That was awesome, wasn't it? It was just what she deserved."

No, it wasn't awesome. It was horrible. The twins are behind Naomi. Skye stares at the sidewalk. Starr glares at me. I get that bad feeling in my gut again. I've tried since Friday to make up with Naomi, but I'm not doing or saying the right thing. My heart beats faster and my feet want to run, but it's time for me to find out the truth.

"Naomi, tell me what I have to do to make you believe that I'm sorry for what happened last Friday. I want to be your best friend again," I say.

She wrinkles her face, and points at me. "You and I will never be best friends again. Don't you realize what you did to me? You backed out on a plan that could give me a shot at being a movie star. How many girls get a chance to be on a television show like *Junior High Spy*? A real best friend would have done everything she could to help me, no matter what. You even pinkie-promised. But you lied. You're not who I thought you were. There's nothing you can do to change my mind."

She tries to walk away, but I touch her arm. "But I did try to help you. And how do you know you're not going to win the tickets? The contest isn't over yet. How could you drop me as your best friend like that? I made one little mistake. I tried to make up for it, but you won't let me." I look her in the eyes. "I would've forgiven you."

Naomi shrugs. "I guess that's where we're different, Mya." Then she nods at the twins. "Let's go, girls."

At that very moment, I know that Naomi and I *are* different, and I don't want to be her friend again. But I'm still not sure if I ever was. Connie's words about Nugget fill my head, and I know I'm taking a big chance here. If I test Naomi, I'd better be ready to accept her answer. If Connie's right, I may never get over it. But if she's wrong, then at least I'll know that at one time, Naomi and I were best friends, and it was real.

I'm breathing faster, moving slower, and I'm absolutely scared to death, but I've got to know. Naomi and the twins move toward the basketball courts.

"Naomi, wait up," I say.

"What now?" she asks with a frown.

"Can I talk with you alone?" I turn to the twins. "I have to ask Naomi something in private."

The twins answer together. "Okay."

"I'm not going to change my mind, so this better be important," says Naomi.

She follows me to an empty area on the playground. I take a deep breath and test her.

"I know you like my brother."

She looks over both shoulders and blushes. "No, I don't."

A lump sits in my throat as big as Mount Everest. This isn't a taradiddle, and I know it. But it's the only way to find out the truth. So I clear my throat and say it.

"What if I can make him like you, too?"

Naomi's eyebrows rise as she stares at me and chews on her bottom lip.

"You can do that?" she asks.

"My brother will do anything I ask him to do," I say, hoping she believes me.

She glances at Nugget playing basketball and then gets in my face.

"Okay. This stays between us, Mya. We can be best friends again, but it doesn't start until Nugget tells me he likes me, got it? He has until tomorrow after school to tell me, or I'll let Connie know, in front of everybody, that you broke the biggest Spirit Week partner rule and that you weren't going to help her win anything. Isn't that what you told me?

Everybody knows that the only thing worse than a promise-breaking cowgirl is a secret-snitching Spirit Week partner."

Her words hit harder than any punch Connie could have given me. I've got enough tears rushing to my eyes to fill the Atlantic Ocean, and I don't know if I'm crying because I'm angry or if it's because I now know the truth, or if I'm crying for Connie. Mr. Winky tweets his whistle, and everybody runs to line up.

I swipe at a tear racing down my face. "We better go before we get in trouble."

My boots feel heavy, like there's water in them, as I walk away from her. My friendship with Naomi is over. It was fake all along and I didn't know it. But the biggest pain comes from knowing how hurt and upset Connie's going to be when she finds out that I did the one thing I promised I wouldn't do.

I double-crossed her.

As my class lines up to go back to class, I take my place at the back. This is where I belong today. I glance at Connie's rubber boot. If I could, I'd kick myself in the rear with it.

Soon, we're moving back inside and toward our class. Everyone runs to the Spirit Week board to find out who won today's costume points, and check out the point leaders.

WEDNESDAY
COSTUME—5 POINTS
David Abrahms and Johnny Collins
CHALLENGE POINTS
DANCE—2 POINTS
Lisa McKinley and Mary Frances Whitaker
SPELLING CHALLENGE—2 POINTS
Skye Falling and Susan Acorn
CAFETERIA ENTERTAINMENT—2 POINTS
Naomi Jackson and Starr Falling

STANDINGS:
Naomi Jackson and Starr Falling—7 POINTS
David Abrahms and Johnny Collins—7 POINTS
Connie Tate and Mya Tibbs—5 POINTS
Skye Falling and Susan Acorn—4 POINTS
Lisa McKinley and Mary Frances Whitaker—
  2 POINTS

I walk back to Connie's desk. She's rolling her eyes. "Those cafeteria talent points should have been ours, Mya. We should be tied with David and Johnny."

My throat hurts from all the words lumped in it. "Connie, can we meet after school?"

"I've got one more poster to make," she says.

I shrug and try not to cry. "Okay. I just have to tell Nugget I'm not walking home with him, and then I'll meet you in the art room."

Chapter Eighteen

After school, I walk down to the art room. The hall seems like it's a mile long. I'm so ashamed of what I've done to Connie that I can't even look at the Spirit Week posters. I knock on the wall since the door to her art room is open. She rinses paintbrushes with one hand and signals me to come in with the other.

"You know, Mya, if we're going to win the VIP tickets, we really need to get the big points tomorrow. David's team and Naomi's team are both beating us by two points. We've got to come up with something extra, over-the-top amazing."

I set my backpack in a chair. "Before we talk about our Spirit Week costumes for tomorrow, I need to tell you something. It's important," I say.

She holds up a hand. "Okay, but let's get the costume for tomorrow figured out first. What do you think about Fire Girls? Our superpower could be that we can set criminals on fire. I can paint both of us red with yellow flames coming off our faces."

My brain shows me what I would look like, and I almost scream. "No, I don't want my face on fire. What about Weather Girls? We can change the weather to help fight crime?"

Connie shrugs. "That's not too bad. Maybe your mom could cover you with a costume that has all four seasons on it. I could paint a T-shirt and put some leaves on it."

I'm too nervous to sit, so I walk over to the GGC and stop. The guardian warriors look so awesome, like crime fighters, like . . .

I spin around to face Connie. "Do they have names?"

Her face lights up. "Of course, and stories, too."

She walks to the first warrior seated on a tall green throne, wearing animal skins and boots made of fur. "This is Animasia, only daughter of Bigfoot and the Lost Princess. She's thirteen years old and guardian of all animals wild and tame, and especially magical animals in the secret woods, like unicorns and stuff."

"If she's guardian over the animals, why is she wearing their skins and furs?" I ask.

Connie cuts her eyes to me. "When the animals shed their skin or fur, they give it to her in a big ceremony to say thanks for keeping them safe and free of hunters."

"That's really cool. Who is that next to her?" I ask.

Connie points to the next guardian. "This is Harmony, daughter of Cupid and the Good Witch. She's guardian of friends and family. Harmony has heart-shaped birthmarks all over and wants everybody to live together in love and peace. She's thirteen, too."

"She's awesome, Connie. Who is that on the Clydesdale?"

"That's Angelica, queen of the GGC. Parents unknown. She's responsible for all the guardian warriors. Queen Angelica is different from the others, but really good at ruling the GGC. Her black crown has the names of all the other guardians engraved in it."

I take a long look at Angelica. Her hair is short

and black. I look back at Connie. Her hair is short and black. Angelica's eyes are blue. So are Connie's. And she's tall! I can tell, even though she's sitting in a saddle. Connie's tall, too.

"Hey, Angelica looks like you."

"No she doesn't," says Connie as she walks to the next warrior.

I giggle and follow her.

"This is Jade-Iris, daughter of Mother Earth and Father Time. Her skin is brown, just like the soil and all the natural things in it. She's the healthiest guardian warrior because she eats nothing but foods grown from the ground. Jade-Iris makes sure everything is done on time, like harvesting and planting, and takes care of all the trees, flowers, and plants. She's thirteen."

I can't help but stare at Jade-Iris. Red, orange, yellow, and purple leaves, with brown twigs, and white flowers cover her body. She's beautiful sitting on that green grassy throne.

"She's the prettiest warrior ever" is all I can say.

Connie stops in front of a young guardian. Gray clouds surround her throne with sprinkles of snow falling from them. Her throne shines as if it's frozen.

"This is Ice, the last guardian warrior in the GGC. She's the only daughter of Mother Nature and Old Man Winter. Ice helps all the other guardians by giving them the weather they need to do their job. She's only ten and doesn't always do what she's told. She's not mean; she just gets frustrated when people don't take care of the planet."

"You made these guardians up all by yourself?" I ask.

Connie nods. "I figured out what they'd wear and what they'd do."

"They're like superheroes or . . ."

I hope she's thinking the same thing I'm thinking, because the GGC is hands down the best group of superheroes ever. If we can win those five points tomorrow for our superhero outfits, maybe Connie won't care that I did something really bad.

She stares at her warriors. "You really think we could do this, Mya?"

I step closer to her, smiling. "Meet me at my house in an hour."

∽

Mom is excited that Connie's coming over. I tell her about the Girl Guardian Court, and what the guardians look like. She gathers material as I talk, and I can tell she's listening by the things she's setting aside for our costumes. She's got wire, glue, and feathers for our wings, along with scissors, pushpins, and a measuring tape.

"I'm going to change clothes. I'll be right back," I say.

Nugget's standing at the top of the stairs. I signal him to come to my room without saying a word. He follows me.

I close my door once we're inside.

"Hey, Nugget, what do you think of Naomi?"

He shrugs. "She's vain, selfish, and rude. Connie has a much nicer disposition. Why do you like Naomi anyway?"

"I don't anymore," I say.

Nugget grins. "Excellent news."

"Did you know she wants to be your girlfriend?" I ask.

He rolls his eyes as his nose wrinkles like he just smelled the world's stinkiest skunk.

"I knew, but I don't like her. Can we talk about something else, because it's quite possible that I miscalculated the negative impact of my friendship with Solo on Fish."

"I'm not sure what you just said, but I think I have one of those problems, too. I can't talk right now, maybe later, okay? Connie's coming over and I need to do something first."

He nods, and opens the door. "Sure. But I really need to talk about this."

Once my brother is gone, I grab the rope off the hook on my wall. My stuffed animals are still on the floor, where I left them a few days ago. Sometimes I do my best thinking when I'm calf roping. I sure hope I can think of a way to tell Connie what I did without her hating me.

It doesn't take long to get a good lasso going. I throw it toward the longhorn.

Missed.

I toss the rope toward the goat.

Missed again.

This rope is horrible! It never lassos anything! I might as well throw it in the trash, because I'm never going to be a good calf roper like Annie Oakley or Cowgirl Claire. I'm never going to ride a Clydesdale. I'm not going to win those VIP tickets, because I'm not even a good Spirit Week partner!

Since the day I picked Connie's name out of that big black hat, she's been the best fake friend I've ever had. Mom likes her. Dad likes her. Even Nugget likes her. I don't know where all those rumors came from or where she got her nickname, but starting tomorrow, I'm going to be as nice to her as she's been to me. And then, when I tell Connie that Naomi wore that Bo Peep outfit because I told her what we were going to wear, maybe she'll forgive me, like a real friend would do.

Chapter Nineteen

Mom's standing at the door with me when Connie comes.

"Hello, queen of hearts! So now you want to be a guardian superhero?" asks Mom.

Connie nods.

"What a perfect choice. Follow me to my magic sewing room."

There's some happy in Connie's walk as she talks to Mom like they've been fake friends forever. Ten minutes later, Connie joins me in the living room.

"Your mom said she should have something

147

ready in about an hour. She's like the fastest seamstress in the universe."

Nugget brings us juice boxes and presses the remote. "You watch *Junior High Spy*?"

"Who doesn't?" she says.

Immediately, my thoughts switch to Naomi. How could she like Nugget more than me?

As I look at Connie, the only thing she's asked me to do is be a good partner. I didn't have to work hard or run home so I could pull out a red bathroom carpet for her to walk on.

Soon Dad comes in. "Hey, kids; oh, I know you! Connie, right?"

"Yes, sir," she says.

On his way to his room, Dad hollers back, "I just saw Naomi. She told me to tell you hello."

Nugget perks up. "Hey, that reminds me. Naomi asked me if I had something to tell her. When I said no, she said I need to talk to you, Mya. What am I supposed to be telling her?"

The whole world goes quiet. I can feel Connie looking at me. Nugget is, too.

I snatch the remote from the table. "Can't we watch something else?"

"You watch *Junior High Spy* every day," says Nugget.

"Not anymore."

"You asked her, didn't you?" says Connie.

I nod.

"Answer my questions. What am I supposed to be telling Naomi, Mya?" asks Nugget.

Connie gets up. "Tell your mom I'll come by later and pick up my costume. I think you need to talk to your brother."

I nod again, trying not to cry. Connie leaves, and now it's just me and Nugget in the room. I tell him what I said, and why I said it. His face is full of anger, but he waits until I finish before saying anything.

"Using me to trap Naomi was wrong. As bad as that was, I still can't believe you broke the biggest Spirit Week rule of all time. Good grief, Mya, you double-crossed Connie. That is the worst thing a Spirit Week partner could ever do. You've got to tell her. She can't find out from Naomi."

I can barely talk. I pull on his shirt. "Help me, Nugget. I don't know how to fix this."

Mom comes out of her sewing room. "Where's Connie? I have her costume in this bag."

Nugget takes the bag from Mom and hands it to me. "Connie had to go home, but Mya said she'd take her the costume as soon as you finished, right, Mya?"

I take the bag from Nugget. My eyes are full of tears, so I don't look at Mom. Instead, I stare at the door. "I'll be right back."

Connie told me she lives on Bayou Bend. I know where that street is. It doesn't take long before I'm standing at the intersection of State Street and Bayou Bend. There are the apartments she must be talking about. I walk to the front, open the door to the main entrance, and see a mailman sorting mail and placing it in the mailboxes. One by one, I check the names on the outsides of the mailboxes. There it is! Tate, J. Apt. 215.

I wait for the elevator since I don't get to ride one that often. After just two knocks, the door opens. Connie's eyes widen.

"Are you okay? Come in. Was Nugget mad at you?"

I hand her the bag. "He was, but you might be even madder. Here's your costume."

"What's wrong?"

Inside, the apartment is small, with the living room and dining room in one area. Paintbrushes and paint cans sit on the table. There's an easel with a tablet of paper sitting near a window in the living room next to a little table with paint and brushes on it. Everything else in the apartment is pushed together just to make room for the paints. The television is on the coffee table. Four TV dinner trays lean against the wall near the fireplace. On the mantel, I count five big trophies.

"Those trophies belong to your dad?"

"They're mine."

I walk toward them. "Are you serious?"

She looks out the window. It takes her a while to answer me. "I don't like to talk about that stuff anymore." Connie points to the sofa. "Sit down over there. I want to know what's wrong. You look terrible. Tell me. Maybe I can help."

I hold up a hand. "Okay."

No more messing around. This is it. I sit on the sofa. She plops down in a chair, and I start with the part she already knows.

"You were right. Naomi likes Nugget. She never really liked me. I should have believed you. I'm sorry."

Her eyes squint as she stares at the ceiling. "I hate her, Mya. I've never told anybody about what she did to me. I wish I had, but I didn't think anybody would believe me."

The mood changes. It's the same feeling I get when dark clouds fill the sky and the wind whistles. Those are signs of a bad storm brewing, and I think there's a hurricane coming right here inside Connie's place.

"How did you know she wasn't my friend?" I ask.

There's a look on Connie's face I haven't seen before. Her eyes are focused on mine. Her lips move, but nothing comes out, and it makes me squirm. Then she points her finger at me, and her face is so serious that I sit up straight.

"What I'm about to tell you is a secret. You have to promise never to tell anyone, not even Nugget."

That scares me. I've got a feeling Connie is about to tell me the juiciest gossip to ever hit Bluebonnet. But it may be news that I don't want to hear. If it is, that will make us even, because I definitely have something to tell her that she won't like.

"So can you keep a secret or not?" she asks again.

I grip the couch cushions and hope for the best. "Tell me. I'm ready."

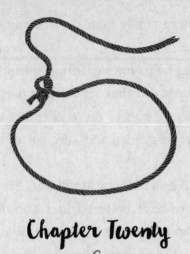

Chapter Twenty

She turns to face me. "All those trophies are from pageants and beauty contests that I've won," says Connie.

I stand and stare at the mantel again. "What? No way!"

She keeps talking. "I went to the same private school as Naomi. My parents don't have a lot of money, and private school is expensive. But my grades were good enough to get a scholarship. It paid for all of my classes, meals, everything. The private school has an art program, and as you probably guessed, I love art."

"And you're really good at it, Connie. That art room is amazing."

"Drawing helps me say things when I can't find the right words. So that school was perfect for me. The only thing I had to do to keep my scholarship was make good grades and stay out of trouble. No problem."

I sit back down and stare at her. Five days ago, I would never have believed that Connie Tate was *not* a troublemaker, and I wouldn't be caught dead sitting in her living room. But now, I've got a feeling she's about to unload some hair-raising, heavy-duty truth on me, and I've made a promise not to repeat it.

Connie folds her arms across her chest. "My mom began signing me up for beauty pageants when I was in second grade."

I almost fall off the couch. "You? I can't imagine you in a beauty contest. I bet you hated it."

"Actually, I loved it! Texas has tons of pageants, so Mom entered me in at least one every month or so. They were a lot of fun. That's when I first became friends with Naomi. We already went to the same private school, but we had different friends and didn't hang out together. Once, we ended up in the same pageant, and she asked me to be her best friend. I said okay. She won that pageant, and

I came in second. I didn't care because I was having so much fun, and I even had a best friend who liked to do the same things I did. We played together, ate lunch together, and even went to the movies together. Things were great until the next pageant."

I let go of the couch cushions. This doesn't sound too bad. "What happened? Did you come in second again?"

She grins. "I almost won!" Then the grin fades away. "That was the problem. The judges liked Naomi's song, but they clapped for a really long time after I showed them the picture I drew. Some of the other contestants thought I was going to take first place. So Naomi asked me to drop out."

My face wrinkles. "What?"

Connie nods. "She said if I was really her best friend, I would drop out of the pageant. I didn't know what to do. I've never quit anything in my whole life, especially a pageant. I told her I didn't want to quit."

There's no doubt in my mind that Naomi was mad at Connie. And I bet she did the same thing to her that she did to me

"So what happened?" I ask.

She chews on her bottom lip. "Every pageant I've been in, when it was time for the talent part,

155

I always drew pictures while music played in the background. That's why I was so angry when Naomi accused me of cheating. She knows I can draw. But anyway, one of the other girls in the pageant asked me if I broke my brother's fingers. I didn't know why she would ask me that, so I told her what really happened. My brother broke his fingers when he fell out of a tree. A few minutes later, another girl in the pageant asked me if I trashed the principal's car. That wasn't true either."

I grip the couch cushions again. I can barely listen.

"But the worst was the rumor that I took my ankle boots off a homeless woman. There are lots more, like painting stripes on my dog, and taking doughnuts back to the bakery for some weird reason. All the girls said Naomi told them the rumors. They believed her because we were best friends. I yelled at Naomi to stop lying about me. That's when she started calling me Mean Connie."

I pound the couch with my fist. "She flipped everything to make it look like you were the mean person when it was really her."

Connie moves from the chair to the sofa, and sits right beside me and pounds the couch, too.

"I was so mad at her for all her lies that I

threatened to beat her up. She told the pageant coordinator and got me kicked out of the competition. Then she told her parents that she was afraid to go back to school because I was going to hurt her. A few days later, the principal gave me an envelope to take home to my parents. It was sealed. I was a good student, Mya, and I had never been in trouble, so I had no idea what the letter said. I thought it was something good! I gave it to my parents. They read it, sat at the table, and stared at each other. I'll never forget the looks on their faces."

Connie gets up, walks over to the mantel, and stares at her trophies. I try to be patient, but the suspense is killing me. When she turns around, her eyes are wet. I'm hurting for her, and I don't even know why yet. But I can tell it's something bad.

"They took away my scholarship, Mya. The letter said the principal had met with the private school committee over a recent incident when I threatened a student. My scholarship was only good as long as my grades were good and I didn't cause any trouble. Because I was a good student, they would allow me to stay if I accepted a one-week suspension, and my parents would have to pay for the rest of the year on the day I came back to school. That was over ten thousand dollars! No way could my parents afford that."

Tears roll down my face and I don't even try to stop them. How can one person be so ugly to so many people, and still win beauty contests?

"Why didn't you tell everybody that the rumors weren't true?" I ask.

She glares at me. "You mean like the way you told everybody that you didn't break your promise on purpose?"

My face warms. I can't look at Connie as I think about all the things I've done to her, when all along, she's the one who deserved to walk on my red bathroom carpet.

And I double-crossed her.

And Naomi Jackson double-crossed me.

Naomi didn't just use me to get Nugget. She used me to get Connie, too.

Now there's no way I can tell Connie what I did. I just can't.

She sits back down. "So that's how I ended up at Young Elementary. Mr. Winky and Mrs. Davis found out about my art talent and asked me if I wanted to do posters for special holidays and school events. I said yes. All the posters you see for Halloween, Valentine's Day, and Spirit Week, I did them.

"Mr. Winky and Mrs. Davis took me down the K3 hall and showed me an empty room. Mr. Winky said if I stay out of trouble, and do a good job on those posters, I can use that room in the back to draw or paint. But if I get in trouble, I lose my art room."

I wipe my eyes and try to smile. "I like your art room, Connie. But I . . . I can't believe what Naomi did to you." I get up and walk to the door. "Tomorrow I'm going to be the best Animasia you've ever seen. And we're going to win those VIP tickets."

Connie smiles. "I think you're going to be an awesome Animasia. You know, I'm glad I didn't agree to trade partners last Friday. You've been a really good Spirit Week partner, Mya, and the best fake friend I've ever had!"

She's still smiling, but I'm dying inside. "I've got to go, Connie. See you tomorrow."

My boots are too heavy and I can't run as fast as I need to. I want to run faster than all the terrible things I've done to Connie Tate. I have to outrun the things Naomi Jackson is going to say to her tomorrow. I've got to stop it all, but I don't know how.

Even though I'll be dressed like Animasia, the best warrior in the Girl Guardian Court, tomorrow may be the worst day of my life because Naomi may tell Connie what I couldn't—that I gave away our secrets, and that I tried to help her win. I may get called names that are worse than Mya Tibbs Fibs. And I'll take the blame for all of it, as long as Connie doesn't get hurt again.

I'm going to do everything I can to make sure it's the perfect day for her.

Chapter Twenty-One

As I walk home, the streetlights buzz to life. It's still light outside, but that's not why I run like the wind toward the house. Mom and Dad have a strict rule about being home by the time the streetlights come on. I open the front door. Mom's there, smiling at me.

"You had me worried for a minute. Is everything okay? Did Connie like the outfit? Did it fit?"

I look for Nugget. His door's closed. That always means he doesn't want to be bothered. I don't know if Connie's costume fits. I don't even know if she likes it. I want to tell Mom what I did, but she doesn't need the stress. Dad's so tired when he gets home from all the work he has to do at the store that I don't want to give him extra drama to handle. Nugget and I promised we wouldn't bother Mom and Dad with our problems unless they were too big for us to figure out on our own. My problem with Naomi and Connie is pretty big, but I'm going to fix everything tomorrow.

I smile and walk toward my room. "Connie's going to be an awesome Queen Angelica."

I stop on the steps and look back to look at Mom. She's still smiling, rubbing her belly, and looking like the most beautiful mom to ever wear house slippers shaped like cowgirl boots. "You really are amazing, Mom. Thanks for helping us with our costumes, and my braids, and everything else."

She stops rubbing her belly. I see a tear in her eye. Good gravy. Now I've made Mom cry, too.

I rush upstairs and close my door. The cows and horses on my wall stare at me. Annie Oakley and Cowgirl Claire give me a look like I need to tell them what I did.

So I do.

I must have fallen asleep, because a knock on my door scares me so badly that I fall on the floor.

I wipe my face. "Who is it?"

"Mom and Dad said it's time for dinner. Come on, let's go," says Nugget.

I *ka-clunk* over to the door and open it. We stand there, staring at each other for a moment, before Nugget reminds me with a whisper, "I'm sure Dad's had a long day at work. Mom and the baby don't need any stress. We'll talk later, okay?"

I nod and follow my brother downstairs. Dad's already at the table, dressed in a clean shirt, holding his knife and fork like he's starving to death. Nugget and I grin at him as we take our places at the table. Mom's made her yummy meat loaf with mashed potatoes and green beans. Nugget and Dad stare at the food and then back at each other.

"Maybe I should get my food first, before you take it all. I'm still a growing boy," says Nugget with a smile.

Dad shrugs. "You might just have to grow someplace else, because that meat loaf is mine."

I can't help but giggle. Mom comes to the table, wiping her hands on her apron.

"If I had known we were going to have a food fight, I would have made spaghetti."

Nugget and I laugh, and Dad joins us.

After Dad gives thanks for our food, Mom starts off by telling us about her day.

"The baby moved a lot, so I had to rest more than I wanted to and that put me behind on the housework. But then I ran out of peanut butter, and it depressed me so bad that I had to take a nap. When I woke up, I realized I had loaded the washing machine but forgot to start it," she says, getting a scoop of mashed potatoes and squirting catsup all over them. My eyes meet Nugget's, and we cover our mouths to hide our grins.

Dad's plate is piled up like he's building a castle. "This should fill my empty stomach," he says. "Today was a long day at the store. I had two people ask for refunds for Bronco Buck Willis stuff they bought last week. Then some little boy pushed the button on the side of Buttercup, and when the bull started bucking, it scared him so badly that he ran through the store knocking over displays, camping gear, all kinds of stuff. I spent my entire lunch hour cleaning up that mess. Right before I left the store, the Fall Festival Committee called and said they're working on a contract for a rodeo replacement, but they wouldn't tell me who it was."

I glance at Dad. "Not even a clue?"

"Not even one lousy clue," he says.

I stab another forkful of meat loaf and shove it into my mouth. Mom takes a long swig of her cranberry juice. "Mya, Nugget, do you know why your father and I are so happy about the new baby?"

I shrug. "New babies are fun," I say.

Nugget looks at Dad. "Another tax deduction?"

Dad laughs. I do, too, even though I have no idea what a tax deduction is.

Mom wipes her mouth, puts both elbows on the table, and props her chin on the backs of her hands. "The reason we're so happy about having another child is because the two we have are so wonderful! Your father and I love being your parents."

Dad nods at me and fist-bumps Nugget as Mom continues.

"Don't think we can't handle your problems. We can, and we want to help."

I slowly let my fork drop on my plate. Nugget's eyes are glued to Mom's as she begins to cry.

"It's so precious of you to try and keep your problems away from your dad and me because you think we can't handle them right now."

Nugget stares at Dad. "You knew?"

My eyes widen. "How'd you know that?"

Dad's eyebrows rise as he nods. "It's been tough on your mom and me, waiting for both of you to come and talk to us. We know when things aren't going well for you. Things don't always go right out there in the world. But in here, at this table, we're family, and we help each other, understand? That's what families do."

Mom holds out her arms. "Come here, Sir Nugget."

Dad holds out his arms. "Come here, baby girl."

I'm almost running to the end of the table. I close my eyes and let Dad hug me. My arms wrap around his neck. His face feels so warm and perfect, just like a dad should feel.

He whispers in my ear. "You can always talk to me, Mya, about anything. You hear?"

"Yes, sir," I say without letting go of his neck.

The dining room is quiet, but it doesn't feel strange. It feels like a whole lot of love in the room, and that's exactly what I needed. And since I don't hear my brother saying anything, I'm thinking that's exactly what he needed, too.

Chapter Twenty-Two

Thursday morning, I wake up scared, shaking, and totally nervous. I already know that today may not be a good day. But I've made up my mind. I've got to tell Connie the truth. She's got to know what I did, even if I have to ask someone else to tell her.

And I've already figured out who can do that for me.

There's a really good reason why I'm not wearing braids today. It's better for my hair to hang down and be free, loose, like animal hair. I tie the bandanna made out of fake leopard skin around my head. My pants are made out of the same leopard-skin material, and they have big belt loops so I can hook my rodeo rope on them. Last night I made two bracelets with green and black beads. It's time to put them on.

As I stare into the mirror, my big guardian wings, covered with the same material as my bandanna and my pants, give me courage and make this costume worth a thousand Spirit Week points. This is the best outfit Mom's ever made.

But right now, I need to switch from the scared me to the brave me. If I'm going to be a superhero, I need to start by telling Connie the truth, and I've failed twice.

But I know who can do it.

I reach down on my dresser, grab my brown cowgirl hat, and gently place it on top of my head, over the bandanna. Slowly I look up and stare at the mirror, because today I am no longer Mya Tibbs.

"Good morning, Animasia," I say to the mirror.

Downstairs, Mom makes a big deal out of the way I look. She's got a peanut butter–and-onion sandwich in one hand as she hugs me with the other. When Dad and Nugget step out of the garage, they take white masks and goggles off their faces.

Nugget is barefoot and dressed in a pair of raggedy brown shorts and a dark-blue shirt, with the rest of his body, including his hair and face, painted dark blue. Mom and I laugh. Nugget flexes his tiny muscles. "Planet Man is in the house!"

"If you're Planet Man, why are you blue?" I ask.

"Our planet is mostly made up of water. My brown pants represent land. I protect both."

Girl Guardian Jade-Iris already has that covered, but I'd never tell Nugget to his face. He puts his shoes on and we leave for school. Just as we cross the street, Nugget breaks the news.

"I'm meeting Solo in front of the school instead of the park. He's Solar System Man. I don't have any idea what his superpowers are supposed to be, but that's what he chose. Anyway, I'm late, so I'm going to run ahead, okay? See you at lunch."

"Whatever," I say.

A few moments later, I hear a familiar voice. "Mya Papaya!"

My smile gets bigger when I see Fish dressed in Superman gear, except he has a big *F* painted on his shirt instead of an *S* for Superman, and fins on his sides. He turns to me, and holds up his hand. "Happy Teddy Bear Day! Whoa, you look awesome!"

"Thanks, Fish, but call me Animasia, Guardian of the Secret Woods. And happy Teddy Bear Day to you, too!"

Fish keeps talking. "Did you know that Teddy Bear Day is named after President Theodore Roosevelt? Check this out. President Roosevelt liked to hunt, but one day he didn't shoot anything. Somebody brought him a real baby bear to shoot, but he wouldn't do it. A toymaker read what happened and brought out a stuffed bear called Teddy's Bear. The rest is history!"

I give Fish his high five. "What a cool story! What's the *F* on your shirt for?"

He slaps his chest. "Meet the Fabulous Fish Man, protector of every fish under the sea!"

I give him another high five for being the best Fish Man in Bluebonnet.

"Bobby Joe is going to be Thunder Boy. He booms so loud that it scares off his enemies," says Fish.

I nod. "Sounds like a great team. I hope you win the big points today."

PSST!

I stop and listen. There it is again.

PSST!

"Animasia! Over here, behind the bushes!"

Ka-clunk, ka-clunk, ka-clunk.

"Who's there?" I ask.

"Queen Angelica." Connie walks out from behind the bushes.

Fish stares. "Connie, you look uh . . . I don't know. Geez, I've never seen you in a dress before. What's the opposite of ugly?"

"Pretty," says Connie with a grin.

Fish nods. "Yep, I agree. See you at lunch." He runs toward school with his fins flapping back and forth.

We yell together. "Bye, Fabulous Fish Man!"

Connie runs her hand across her long dress, then looks back at me.

"I'm not wrinkly, am I?"

"No, you look perfect," I say. "But I need to talk to you about—"

Connie puts her hands up. "Please. Don't say anything else, Animasia. Whatever you have to tell me can wait. This is the most perfect morning I've had in two whole years. I even feel like Queen Angelica! Let's just walk to school together, okay?"

Good gravy.

I nod. "Okay. Let's go."

We walk to school, side by side, in silence. Students stare at us, smile at us, wave at us, some even speak to us. But we stay silent, focused. Like warriors. Today, Animasia and Queen Angelica are real superheroes.

Finally we reach Mr. Winky. Nugget's standing at the door beside him.

"Where's Solo," I ask.

Nugget shrugs. "He didn't show up, so I thought I'd wait on you guys. That outfit is boo-yang cool, Connie."

She finger-combs her hair. "Seriously? Thank you."

Mr. Winky's dressed like some jungle man with a fake monkey on his shoulder. He beats his chest when we approach and hollers like Tarzan.

"AAAAWWWWAAAWWWAAAA."

He points at my brother. "Me, Winky Man. You, Nugget Man!"

I pet the monkey on his shoulder and think about freeing it since I'm Animasia today.

"Cool outfit, Mr. Winky," says Connie.

He points at Connie and me, and then switches back to a Mr. Winky voice.

"Take a look at the two superheroines. Absolutely beautiful! Yes, yes, yes! It doesn't matter if you're super 'he'-roes or super 'she'-roes; we're having a super Spirit Week at Y.E.S.!"

I'm so proud to be standing next to Connie. She

doesn't look like Mean Connie Tate. Right now, she looks like the prettiest girl in Bluebonnet. "Let's go," I say. "We've got to model our outfits down the K3 hall. They're going to love them!"

Just as we turn the corner, we see Starr taking a picture of Naomi near the water fountain. We both stand as still as statues while Naomi gawks at Connie. Never in my wildest dreams would I have imagined this happening.

Crowds of kindergarteners and first, second, and third graders look at Connie, then at Naomi. Students fill the hallway and I can hear the whispers.

Naomi has wings. So do Connie and Mya.

Naomi frowns. "Who are you supposed to be, Connie? I'm the Angel of Beauty. I change ugly things into beautiful things."

I roll my eyes. "More like the Angel of Cootie."

Connie pushes my shoulder. "Cool it."

Naomi ignores me. She's eyeballing Connie, frowning.

"You remember what happened the last time you tried to be better than me?"

As I glare at my ex–best friend, she seems to get uglier by the second. After hearing Connie's story yesterday, I could just walk over to Naomi and rip her wings off. I can't let her ruin Connie's chances of winning again, like she did in the pageant.

I've had enough of Naomi Jackson. I'm tired of her being mean to me and my Spirit Week partner. It has to stop, and I'm going to stop it right now.

Today, I'm Animasia. My job is to protect my queen.

I step in front of Connie and stand strong. "Let me handle this."

Chapter Twenty-Three

The crowd keeps growing, but I've got only one thing on my mind. I raise my hands and speak loud enough for everyone to hear. "I am Animasia, guardian over all animals in the Secret Woods. Citizens of Young Elementary, I give you Queen Angelica, leader of the Girl Guardian Court. You should bow to her."

Some of the first, second, and third graders take a knee, but Naomi scares them.

"Don't bow to her! Connie couldn't be queen of anything! She doesn't know how!"

"Wrong, Queen Cootie! You're the one who's

fake, phony, and full of baloney," I say.

Connie frowns and pushes my shoulder again. "No name calling!"

Naomi hollers at me. "Why do you care? You don't even like Mean Connie Tate!"

"Stop calling her that! Her name is Queen Angelica," I say.

Naomi steps closer to me. "Mean Connie needs to hear the truth."

I fight back with a whisper only she needs to hear. "You're just mad because you like my brother, but he doesn't like you."

I know those are fighting words, but it's the only thing I could think of to say to make Naomi leave Connie alone. Naomi's eyes squint, her nose wrinkles, and I know she's about to blow. In my head, I encourage myself to be strong. *I am a warrior. I am Animasia. Naomi Jackson can't hurt me anymore. I won't let her. And I won't let her hurt my queen.*

Naomi points at me. "So, Mean Connie, you think you know your Spirit Week partner?"

Connie frowns at her. "I don't think I do; I know I do!"

I bump fists with Connie for joining in the fight, but it's far from over. The fear I had this morning is trying to come back. I tell myself again to be strong.

I am a warrior. I am Animasia . . .

Good gravy. It's not working.

Naomi smiles at Connie. "You're such a sucker. Mya totally double-crossed you."

I quickly turn to Connie. "Please, you have to listen to me. I have to tell you something before it's too late!"

Connie looks down at me. I look up, and her eyes seem to ask why this is happening. I'm sure mine are asking for forgiveness.

Naomi's almost in between us. "Connie, why do you think I was dressed like Bo Peep on Tuesday? It's because your Spirit Week partner told me what you and her were going to wear. She even offered to tell me other things if I would take her back as my best friend."

Connie fires back. "I don't believe you, Jackson. I know Mya and she wouldn't do that."

Sirens, bells, whistles, fire, ice, rocks, everything loud, everything painful, is beating, slicing, twirling, and destroying my insides like the world's worst battle. It's over. All I can do is stand here, in the middle of the hall, while Naomi trashes me in front of the whole school.

"Mya Tibbs is a Spirit Week snitch! She told me and my partner everything she and Connie were going to do for Spirit Week."

Connie taps me on the shoulder. "Mya, you told her about the GGC?"

My body thumps with fear. "No! She's lying!"

Connie stomps her foot. "I don't believe you, Jackson! Mya's not like that."

Connie's fighting for me. She's fighting for our friendship. But Naomi just smiles. Those green eyes of hers that I used to believe were so beautiful now twinkle evil. Then she comes back with a bigger lie—one that I didn't see coming, and can't defend against.

"It's totally true. Why else would I be wearing an angel costume like yours?"

Connie looks at Naomi's dress and then her own. Slowly she faces me. I don't have an answer, so I shrug and guess. "Maybe she was spying on us, or maybe it's just by chance that she's dressed like an angel—you know, like a coincidence—but I swear I didn't tell her."

Connie sends me a stink eye that I can almost smell. "First, you gave away our Bo Peep idea. And then you did it again? You dirty double-crossed me . . . Tibbs."

She called me Tibbs. Oh no. I step closer to her. "It's true that I told her about Bo Peep, but that was all! I didn't tell her about the GGC! I didn't tell her about today, I swear!"

Naomi interrupts me. "Don't listen to her, Connie. She's the biggest liar in Bluebonnet."

Connie bolts down the hall. The wings on the back of her costume flap like she's going to leave the ground. I know where she's going, but I'm not finished with Naomi.

"*You're* the biggest bully in this school, not Connie," I say.

Naomi stares down the hall. "I bet she's on her way to go scare the poor kindergarteners."

"No she's not!"

Naomi crosses her arms. "How do you know, Mya Tibbs Fibs? She's probably changed you into a bully, too! There's no other reason for her to go down that hall."

I frown. "Yes there is! If it weren't for Connie, we wouldn't have all these awesome posters for Spirit Week. She painted all of them!"

Everybody checks out the posters. I hear them whispering. *"Mean Connie drew this?" "No way!" "Maybe Connie did draw that picture during the talent challenge in the cafeteria!"*

I keep talking. "Yeah! And that's not all. She's got a room full of awesome things she's created. She's got more talent in her fingers than Naomi Jackson has in her whole body!"

"Mean Connie's got her own art room? I need to see this! Come on, hurry, everybody," says Naomi.

Somebody pushes me against the wall. Students shove by. Others run.

It's a stampede.

I've ruined everything. If only these wings were real, I'd fly away and never come back. What am I saying? I'm Animasia! I'm supposed to protect Queen Angelica, no matter what. I can't protect her leaning against this wall. I take a deep breath and shout down the hall.

"Stay away from Queen Angelica's castle, Naomi! Stop!"

I'm at the back, pushing, trying to get through. "Move, please. Excuse me."

Naomi's leading the herd. I can't let her trash Connie's art room. I can't let all these kids push their way inside and knock over her paints, and break her colored chalk. It will crush her. But worst of all, she'll blame me for snitching again.

I don't have much time left. It's now or never.

I yell one last time. "Naomi, leave her alone!"

She holds up a fist. "You can't stop me, Mya Tibbs Fibs!"

I have to do something, but what can I do? I try to run faster, but my arm keeps banging against something on my costume. I look down.

Jambalaya!

I pull my rodeo rope off of my belt loop, close my eyes, kiss my rope, and then talk to it.

It's up to us. Don't miss.

I make the best lasso I can, then shout at the crowd. "Get out of my way!"

For the first time since I stopped being popular, students move, open up a clear path, and watch as the rope glides through the air. I belt out a rodeo yell. "Yippee-ki-yay!"

The loop drops over Naomi and down to her waist. I pull it tight. "Gotcha!"

"Hey, what's going on? Where did this rope come from?" yells Naomi.

The crowd stops and watches Naomi wiggle to get loose.

"Let go of me, Mya Tibbs Fibs!" she screams. "Skye, go get Mrs. Davis!"

I dash over to Naomi and tackle her to the floor,

and as I rope her arms and legs together, I count it off—"One, two, three, four"—then throw my hands into the air.

Starr and Skye rush to me and check their watches. I hear them talking to each other.

"Four seconds is fast," says Skye.

"Blazing fast," says Starr.

"Got her on the first try, too," says Skye.

"On the very first try," say Starr.

I yell to the crowd. "Four seconds! It's a new Bluebonnet rodeo record!"

Students clap and whistle, ignoring Naomi screaming on the floor, hog-tied and helpless. I take my hat off and bow to the crowd. "Call me Animasia, Girl Guardian over all animals wild and tame in the Secret Woods, and protector of Queen Angelica."

Naomi yells at Starr. "I said go get Mrs. Davis!"

The twins frown. I don't know if anyone else can see it, but to me, they're glowing. Maybe it's the sun shining through the windows. Maybe it's how they look when they're angry.

Or maybe they really are aliens.

Skye disappears into the crowd. Starr leans over Naomi. "It took Mya four seconds to tie you up. Let's see how long it takes you to get loose! One, two, three, four, five . . ."

Fish Man pats me on the back. "Nice job, Animasia."

"Thanks, Fabulous Fish Man," I say.

Down the hall, Connie stands at her door. I hold my fist in the air. "Hail to the queen!"

Fish lifts his books. Others lift books, backpacks, fists, jackets, whatever they have, and shout, "HAIL TO THE QUEEN!"

Connie puts her fist over her heart, and I bow. Fish drops down to one knee. Others do the same. Holy firecrackers.

Naomi hollers again. "She is *not* a queen! Untie me, Mya Tibbs Fibs!"

Starr's still counting. "Twenty-two, twenty-three, twenty-four . . ."

Nugget shows up. "Whoa! I've never seen a Junior Miss Lone Star get calf roped before. I'd ask for your autograph, but you seem to be a bit tied up at the moment."

Solo pushes his way through and tries to untie Naomi. He glares at Nugget. "Dude, what's wrong with your sister? She's crazy, just like Connie! They're both losers."

Suddenly, Solo topples over Naomi's tied-up body. Fish Man stands over him. "Don't ever call

Animasia and the queen losers again, Solo!"

Starr breathes out a mouthful of air. "Sixty-seven, sixty-eight, sixty-nine . . ."

A whistle blows. I know Mrs. Davis's whistle when I hear it. Fabulous Fish Man grins, then rushes off into the sunset like all heroes do. Solo scrapes himself off the ground and runs, too. Nugget stands with me. There's no way I can untie Naomi before Mrs. Davis sees her.

I don't care. I defended my queen. I protected her castle. I did my job.

But now, I'm in big, big trouble.

Chapter Twenty-Four

Naomi glares at Starr while she counts. "Eighty-eight, eighty-nine, ninety . . ."

Nugget cracks his knuckles. "I was going to do something, Mya, but Fish beat me to it."

I won't look at him. "I don't need any help, Nugget. I know what I'm doing."

"I should've . . . Never mind." He dashes away before my teacher reaches me.

As she gets closer, Mrs. Davis's mouth opens but nothing comes out. Starr and I are the only two students left, besides Naomi squirming on the floor like a worm on a fishing hook.

Finally, Mrs. Davis's voice comes in. "Mya, are you responsible for this?"

I grin. "Roped her in less than five seconds. Got her on the first try, too!"

Mrs. Davis stares at me. There's only one more thing I want to do.

"I'm sure Naomi will want a picture for her portfolio. Can we take one before I untie her? We can use her cell phone. She keeps it in her purse."

From the look on our teacher's face, we're not going to take a picture. As soon as I finish untying Naomi, Starr checks her watch. "One hundred and twelve seconds. Geez, Naomi, that's embarrassing. I can't wait to tell Skye."

"Starr, get to class. Where's your sister?" asks Mrs. Davis.

"I don't know. She was here a minute ago."

Mrs. Davis helps Naomi up. "Do you want to go see the nurse?"

She frowns. "No, but Mya needs to get kicked out of school for what she did to me."

Naomi storms off, yelling for Starr to wait up. I look for Skye but don't see her. I've never seen the twins apart unless one was in Mr. Winky's office. Something's wrong.

Mrs. Davis folds her arms across her chest. "This

is not like you, Mya," she says.

I look down the hall toward the art room. "I was just taking up for my friend."

Mrs. Davis frowns. "You take up for friends by calf roping them?"

For the first time, it doesn't matter what people think of me. I don't care what they say. I'm ready to let the world know. "I was talking about Connie Tate."

The expression on Mrs. Davis's face changes. I can tell she's surprised, but in a good way. "Oh, I see. Come on. We have to go," she says.

It's a long *ka-clunk* to Mr. Winky's office. The first bell rings, and students rush to clear the hallway. I should have more giddyup in my steps, but I don't. I'm in no hurry to see the principal.

Inside the main office, there are five chairs against the wall outside of Mr. Winky's door. "Wait here while I talk with the principal," says Mrs. Davis.

"Yes, ma'am."

Rrrring!

"Good morning, Young Elementary School, how can I help you?"

Mr. Winky's secretary is dressed like Wonder Woman. She glares at me, and then at the clock, probably wondering how I managed to get in trouble before the Pledge of Allegiance.

I wish the clock would be quiet. That ticking is so loud. *Tick, tick, tick.*

"Okay, I'll let Donald's teacher know he's sick. Good-bye." says the secretary. *Swish . . . swish . . . swish.*

Who's using the copying machine this early in the morning? It's too loud!

Rrrring!

"Good morning, Young Elementary School, how can I help you?"

Tick, tick, tick.

Swish . . . swish . . . swish.

All the ticking and swishing and ringing and staring is making me nervous.

Mrs. Davis opens the door. "Okay, Mya. Come in."

Mr. Winky sits behind his big desk in his jungle man costume with the stuffed monkey on his shoulder. He's tapping a pen on the glass top as I walk in. I've never seen Mr. Winky in a bad mood, but I think that's what he's in right now since he's not smiling at me or saying yes, yes, yes about something. He closes his eyes and speaks to me.

"Mya, Mya, Mya. I never thought you'd be in my

office for bullying. Oh no, no, no. But here you are, dressed like a superhero, yet behaving like a villain."

"I didn't bully anybody, Mr. Winky," I say.

Mrs. Davis sits beside me. "Calf roping another student definitely falls into the category of bullying, even if your intentions were good."

"And you've now left Connie Tate without a Spirit Week partner," says Mr. Winky.

He doesn't know that I've left Connie without a *good* Spirit Week partner for most of this week. I deserve whatever punishment I get.

Mrs. Davis interrupts my thoughts. "Mya, we have decided that you will spend the rest of your day in in-school detention."

"In-school detention? Isn't that like . . . student jail? I need a lawyer."

Mr. Winky leans over his desk. "It's either in-school detention or three days' suspension. Your choice, Mya."

"I'll take jail."

"Unfortunately, I have to call your parents," says Mrs. Davis.

"Please call my dad. Mom's going to burp out a baby soon. I don't want to upset her."

"Okay, that's fair. I'll call your father," she says.

189

Mr. Winky speaks up. "Because of your inexcusable behavior, you will not be allowed to participate in Decorate Your Cubby or Cabinet Day tomorrow, and unfortunately, you and Connie are disqualified from winning the Fall Festival VIP tickets."

If Mr. Winky was looking for the one thing that would hurt me the most, he found it. "Don't punish Connie. Everything was my fault, not hers," I say.

Mr. Winky shrugs. "The Spirit Week rules are set up to give points to a team of two. How's she going to win points without a partner?"

I plead with him as I lean over his desk. "But she didn't do anything wrong."

He points his pen at me. "You should have thought about that before you broke the rules."

That's it. My legs give out. I fall back into my chair, cover my face and cry so hard that my head hurts. Just when I didn't think I could make matters worse, I did.

Mrs. Davis touches my shoulder. "Come on. I'll take you to the detention room."

I *ka-clunk* down the hall, sniffling and wiping my nose on the sleeve of my costume. We pass the cafeteria, the restrooms, the water fountain, and Mrs. Davis's room. I sneak a look inside. The librarian is reading a story, and everyone seems to be listening. Connie's at her desk. She's still dressed in her Queen Angelica costume. There are Skye and Starr, and Naomi.

Mrs. Davis calls to me. "Let's go, Mya."

Ka-clunk, ka-clunk, ka-clunk.

Mrs. Davis unlocks a door at the very end of the hall. It's dark inside and smells like air freshener. She flips on the light, and there's nothing in the room but empty desks, each one facing the wall with dividers in between them.

I need those sad country-and-western songs I downloaded last weekend.

Mrs. Davis points to a desk in the middle. "Over there, Animasia."

I'm no longer Animasia. Now I'm Detention-asia.

Mrs. Davis crosses her arms. "The rules are simple: No talking, not even to yourself. Someone will bring you your books and assignments. You will eat your lunch in here. I will come by every hour for you to use the restroom and get a quick drink from the fountain. Do you have any questions?"

"No, ma'am."

"Then have a seat. Someone will bring you your homework soon."

Once Mrs. Davis closes the door, the room becomes a lot bigger than it was when I first walked in. Even the quiet is loud. I try singing "She'll Be Roping All the Cattle When She Comes." Mrs. Davis said no talking; she didn't say anything about singing. I sing until I'm sick of the song, then glance at the clock. Only fifteen minutes have gone by.

I wonder what Annie Oakley or Cowgirl Claire would think of me if they saw me locked up in the school jail. I'm so mad at myself that I wish I could step out of my skin and leave it here while I return to my life two weeks ago. Everything was fine, perfect, awesome. I put my elbows on the desk and cry again. The door creaks. I stay still and face the wall because I don't want the office worker to see me crying.

"Mrs. Davis asked me to bring you your stuff."

I know that voice.

Connie.

We love
Sprit Week "Beary"
much!

Chapter Twenty-Five

I point to a desk against a different wall. "You can put my stuff over there. Thank you."

I hear the books plop on a desk, and then Connie clears her throat. "Mrs. Davis thinks she put too much pressure on us to be friends. I told her it wasn't her fault that you're a no-good, dirty-double-crossing Spirit Week partner. Did you know we got disqualified? Thanks a lot."

I don't know why I'm dead-red mad, but I am. "I made a big mistake, but I tried to make it right. We got disqualified because I was trying to protect your castle! Besides being disqualified, I got completely kicked out of Spirit Week! I don't even get to decorate my cabinet tomorrow. And when I get home, I'm going to get sent to my room for the rest of the night. I'll probably get grounded."

I refuse to look at her even though I know she's still standing there because I didn't hear the door close. But I do hear her clearing her throat.

"Even though we're disqualified, Mr. Winky chose me to be in the character parade today. I'm the only angel. Fish made it, too."

I know that's her way of telling me that Naomi didn't get chosen. But right now, I'm in the worst mood ever. "Well, whoop-de-doo! *Some of us* won't get to see the parade because *some of us* are stuck in the school jail."

I hear the door open, then close. At first I think she's gone but then I hear her voice again.

"I saw you tie up Naomi. You really are a good roper, but you're a terrible friend."

I holler at her. "Well, maybe you're a terrible friend, too!"

Connie hollers back. "Why am I a terrible friend? You're the one who snitched! You double-crossed me, Tibbs."

I don't know why it bothers me that she calls

me Tibbs again, but it does. Maybe it's because I liked how she said my name, like a real friend. And I know, even if she never calls me Mya again, she deserves to hear the truth from me.

I hold up one finger. "I didn't tell her about our outfits today, Connie." I hold up a second finger. "And I didn't tell her about the GGC. That's two things Naomi lied about."

Connie nods. "I know. After you calf roped Jackson, Skye snuck over to the art room and told me that she lied. But you're still just like her."

I've heard enough. If she pulls my lips off and sticks them to the wall, then I'll just have to peel them off and put them back on. But I'm not going to let her talk to me like that.

"I'm not the one who's like Naomi Jackson. You are, Connie! I made a really bad mistake, but real friends, maybe even fake friends, would say, 'I know you didn't mean it' or 'let it go' or 'I forgive you,' but you didn't. Neither did Naomi. I'm in detention because I was trying to be your friend, your best friend, because I thought maybe you were trying to be mine."

We're staring at each other again, just like we did out in the hall on the day I picked her name.

Tears roll down my face. Connie wipes her eyes with the back of her hand.

She opens the door. "I've got to get back to class."

When the door closes, the sound echoes in the room, reminding me that I'm alone again. I wipe the tears away so that I can see my way over to the desk where Connie put my books. There's a handwritten page on the top. It's from Mrs. Davis.

Mya,

>*You've had a very rough morning. Below are your reading assignments and class work. I hope that tomorrow is a better day for you.*

>>*Mrs. Davis*

Here I am, almost at the end of the one week in the whole school year that I look forward to, and it all got canceled.

Mr. Winky canceled my Spirit Week.

Connie canceled our friendship.

Mom and Dad are going to cancel everything fun in my life.

The way I see it, tomorrow doesn't matter. I lost everything I cared about today.

∽

I sat so long in detention that my butt tingles and my wings are bent. I can't walk home any faster, but if I could, I would.

"Are you okay, Mya?" asks Nugget, almost running to keep up.

"Leave me alone," I say.

All I want to do is get my punishment, go to my room, and listen to sad music. Mom greets me at the door eating a Cobb burger from the Burger Bar.

"Hello, Mya. I know you've had a bad day. Your father said he would handle everything when he gets home, and you're to go straight to your room."

"Yes, ma'am."

As I walk away, she pulls me back and hugs me. "No matter what, I love you."

"Thanks, Mom."

I dash up the steps to my room. Jiggling my shoulders makes the backpack slide down my arms, and I slam it on my bed, making some of the stuffed animals bounce from my pillow to the floor. I pick up the stuffed goat, the cow, even the horse, and throw them one at a time against the wall. There's an old doll sitting on my shelf. I grab her by the hair and swing her around and around until I don't want to anymore. There are those stupid unlucky boots. I kick them, and then kick them again. I yank at the wings on my back. The material rips and I keep yanking.

Knock, knock.

I open the door, sweating, out of breath, one wing touching the floor, and still holding that doll by her hair. My brother stands in front of me, crying and sniffling, holding a basketball.

Nugget never cries.

Even when he gets in trouble, he takes it like a tough bull rider. I open my door wider. He walks in and stops in front of my window with his back to me, but I hear him sniffling. I *ka-clunk* over to him.

"I'm listening," I say.

"Solo thinks he's Kevin Durant or LeBron James or some NBA superstar like that, dribbling the ball between his legs and behind his back. He even scored four three-pointers!"

I shrug. "That's good, isn't it? What's the problem?"

Nugget's lips tighten. "He ignored me, as if I was irrelevant. He didn't share the basketball, not one time. Granted, I'm not very good . . ."

More tears fall down his face. "But I try so hard, Mya."

"I know," I say.

Nugget wipes his face. "After recess all he talked about was his exceptional skills. He said I should be happy that he hangs out with me, and then you know what he did?"

I'm too scared to ask, so I just keep listening.

"He called me Word Nerd Nugget. For no reason! I couldn't believe it! I thought Solo would be different, but he's just like all of the other guys, except Fish."

I stand closer to my brother. He's hurting and I know it. I put my arm around his shoulder.

Nugget sniffles. "I sacrificed Spirit Week with Fish for him, and worse, I didn't take up for you when Solo called you a loser. Fish did what I should've done. When I tried to tell him thanks, he walked away from me. I can't believe I've been such a horse's patootie."

My shoulders droop, too. "You're not the only patootie in the room."

We stand at the window saying nothing. Then he balls his fists and punches the air. "I should have popped Solo in the eye when he called you a loser. You're not a loser, Mya; I'm the loser, for not taking up for my sister."

He hugs me, and I let him. "I'm really sorry," he says.

I needed to hear that.

"I know you didn't mean it," I say. When he lets

go, I grab an old rodeo rope from the toy box since Mr. Winky's got my good one. I twirl it and think out loud.

"Okay, so what do you want to do?"

He stares at me. "I want my best friend back. I want Fish to talk to me."

I point at him. "Good. First you need to tell Fish you're sorry for being a big jerk. Then, play whatever he wants to play at recess to prove to him that he's your best friend. What kind of games does he like to play? And maybe you need to set Solo straight once and for all."

Nugget rubs his forehead and lets his hand slide down his cheek to the back of his neck like a washcloth. "Fish likes to play catch. Baseball is his number-one favorite sport."

I smile and nod. "Now you're thinking!"

Nugget paces again. "I'll get my glove, ask Dad for his, and take them to school. Then I'll surprise him at recess. I sure hope it works." He crosses his arms. "Was it horrible in detention? Connie told me Mr. Winky took away your Spirit Week activity for tomorrow."

I nod. "Took my rodeo rope, too. Spirit Week is over for me. We got disqualified."

My brother hugs me for a long time. "What a

rotten day. I'm sorry, Mya."

I shrug. "And now Connie hates me."

He walks to my door. "Did she say that to your face? Maybe you're wrong. If I get a chance to help you with Connie, I will. See you in the morning."

I change out of my Animasia outfit and put on a pair of last year's pajamas that I don't like anymore because I don't want to waste a good pair on a bad day. An hour later, Dad knocks.

"Mya?"

He's got two bowls of soup and two glasses of Kool-Aid on a tray. We sit at my computer desk and eat while I tell him what happened. Occasionally he rubs his eyes and blinks slowly. One time he falls asleep and I have to nudge him. His red T-shirt is so dirty. He's got pieces of wood shaving in his hair. His face has speckles of paint on it. I feel bad that he had to climb the stairs. After he's worked all day at the store, I know he's tired. It makes me feel worse than detention.

We finish eating and Dad gives me a hug. "Did you not believe me last night at dinner? I know I look tired and beat down when I get home from work, but I always leave a little extra in me for you. I wish you would've spoken with me before you thought calf roping a classmate would be a good solution to a problem. Someone could have gotten seriously hurt."

"It may not seem like it was a good solution right now, but it felt perfect earlier today," I say, and then stare at my empty bowl. "After I had time to think about it in detention, I know I was wrong."

Dad wipes something off my face with his napkin. "You made a mistake. Some mistakes are bad mistakes. Some are honest mistakes. Everybody makes them, Mya, but try to do better, okay?"

I nod and look very serious. "I'm sorry, Dad. I'll make better mistakes tomorrow."

He looks at the ceiling for a long time and then grins at me. "That's my girl. I think you've learned your lesson. Since you spent the day in detention, and you've been in your room all afternoon and evening, I think that serves as enough punishment. See you in the morning for another shot at it, okay?"

Dad hugs me, the same way he hugged me last night. And I hug him back the same way.

Maybe that's what I'll do to Connie tomorrow. I'll ask her for another shot at being friends or Spirit Week partners or whatever she wants. If I'm lucky, she'll forgive me.

Chapter Twenty-Six

"How many braids this morning, Mya?" asks Mom.

"Just shave my head until it's bald," I say.

She walks around the chair to face me. "Are you okay?"

"I'm okay. Two braids are fine. Were you able to get that blue paint off my vest yet?"

"Still working on it," she says.

Geez.

Nugget's late to the breakfast table, but when he comes downstairs, he looks like a pro in his Dallas Mavericks jersey, matching shorts, headband, wristbands, and light-blue Nike shoes. He struts like he's a real NBA player and then takes a deep bow in front of Mom.

"Greetings and salutations, my lady."

She curtsies. "Greetings, Sir Nugget."

"No need to tell me I look good. I already know. I bet Fish will wear his Dallas Mavericks gear today, because it's his favorite team too." He looks my way, and the happy in him goes away.

"Hey, Mya."

"Hey."

After breakfast, I'm in no big hurry to get to school. Today is just a plain ol' Friday since Mr. Winky said I couldn't participate in Decorate Your Cubby or Cabinet Day. I'm only going because I don't want to watch Mom eat those funky sandwiches. I look over my shoulder and see Fish walking slowly. I yank on Nugget's sleeve.

"Here he comes. Do something."

Nugget was right about Fish. He's wearing his Mavericks jersey. I keep looking for Connie, but she's not back there.

"I'm going to walk ahead of you. Hope things work out for you guys," I say.

Nugget pops his knuckles. "Wait, Mya. What if

he becomes angry or irrational? What if he won't talk to me?"

I shrug. "He's your best friend. You'll figure it out."

Ka-clunk, ka-clunk, ka-clunk.

This will probably be the longest day in the history of Spirit Week Fridays. Suddenly, I hear Fish yelling at Nugget, but Nugget isn't yelling back. I wonder if I should run back and try to help. Just as I take a step their way, Nugget pulls two baseball gloves and a ball from his backpack. Fish stops yelling. Now Nugget is talking. Moments later, I watch Fish give my brother a fist bump.

I *ka-clunk* toward school, grinning as if that were Connie and me.

Mr. Winky's at the door. "Mya, I hope you have an extra awesome day today."

Easy for him to say. He's the one who took away my Spirit Week yesterday, dressed in a Tarzan costume with a fake monkey on his shoulder. But I'd never say that to his face.

"Thank you, Mr. Winky."

As I walk down the hall, it's clear that Decorate Your Cubby or Cabinet Day is a big success, because there are only a few students in the halls. Everyone must be inside their classrooms, checking out the decorations.

I walk into my classroom and head straight for the Cave. It's so crowded in there that I can't get in. There's even kids in the Cave who aren't in our class! What's going on in there? I hear someone mention my name.

"Here comes, Mya."

I slow down, almost to a complete stop. Oh no, not again. I can't get in anymore trouble. Naomi Jackson just doesn't know when to quit. There are the twins, staring at me and standing very close together as if they're hiding something, or someone. Skye's grinning. So is Starr.

I take my backpack off my shoulders. "Hi, Skye, hi, Starr. I don't want any more trouble. I just want to put my things away, okay? Could you move please so I can—"

The crowd splits, and now I'm standing directly in front of my cabinet. I blink several times, step closer, and exhale without inhaling first. Just to be sure, I check the name on the door.

It's mine.

My knees won't bend. The Cave is bedtime quiet as I stare at the painted face of Annie Oakley on my cabinet door. She sits high on her horse, waving her western hat with her left hand, smiling at me as if she knew I was coming.

She's wearing pink cowgirl boots and a brown leather vest. There's a bright yellow sun in the painting, a clear blue sky, and a bunch of green mountains with eagles flying at the peaks. Wild horses run from my cabinet to the one next to mine, where cows graze in a field of fruit, Popsicles, and candy. Not far away is a covered wagon covered in skulls.

But that's not all.

Painted on the cabinet door next to mine is an artist sitting in front of an easel, painting with her left hand. Her right hand stretches out to touch Annie Oakley's outstretched hand.

I stare at the painting and think back to when I was at Connie's house, and what she said to me. *Drawing helps me say things when I can't find the right words.*

That's not a Spirit Week partner painting.

That's a message to me from my friend!

I run as fast as I can to the art room. The light is on. She's putting away paintbrushes. Messy spots of blue, red, green, yellow, and brown paint are all over her apron, face, fingers, and arms. I speak first.

"I don't think anybody in the history of Young

Elementary School has ever had a cabinet or cubby look that awesome. I'm so, so sorry for double-crossing you."

She nods. "I owe you an apology, too. I thought about what you said to me yesterday when you were stuck in jail. I don't want to be like Naomi Jackson. And even though you double-crossed me, I had more fun this week than I've had in two years."

I'm so happy I could do flips! "So you're not mad about the VIP tickets?"

Connie smiles. "Nope. Maybe we can have fun standing in those long lines together."

I get chill bumps. "I don't mind standing in long lines," I say. "And this year, I'm tall enough for all the good rides."

"Good. We'll ride them together," says Connie.

I walk toward the art room door. "See you in class."

"Okay, Mya."

There's still a crowd around my cabinet when I get there. Skye and Starr walk up to me. Naomi isn't with them. Skye takes my hand. "I don't like not being your friend, Mya."

"Really don't like it," says Starr.

"But we like Naomi, too," says Skye.

"She's our friend," says Starr.

"So sometimes we'll hang out with her, and sometimes we'll hang out with you, okay?"

"We'll split our time," says Starr.

Reason number seven on my list of proof that the twins are aliens.

They can figure out how to be friends with two people who are enemies.

I smile. "That's fine with me."

Starr hugs me. "Cool."

"Very cool," says Skye with a smile.

"Thank you," I say. "We'd better get to class."

We stroll out of the Cave and into our classroom. "Good morning, Mrs. Davis."

"Right back at you, Mya. I saw your cabinet. It's beautiful."

I nod. "Yep. My friend has lots of talent."

Mrs. Davis grins. "Yes, your friend does."

Last week, *school bully* and *friend* were as far away from my lips as Texas is from China. Now, they're together, causing a new rhythm in my *ka-clunk*. The yippee is back in my ki-yay and it's all because of Connie Tate.

Chapter Twenty-Seven

After the Pledge of Allegiance, Mr. Winky continues. "It's a beautiful day at Y.E.S., yes, yes it is. I hope everybody is having a wonderful Spirit Week. This afternoon, I'm excited to give VIP tickets for the Fall Festival to the best Spirit Week partners in each grade. You've all worked so hard, and had so much fun! So teachers, after the fourth- and fifth-grade recess, please bring your classes to the cafeteria for our Spirit Week assembly. Thank you!"

Ten minutes later, the sound of big trucks rolling down the street fills our room. I don't think anyone is paying attention to Mrs. Davis. Finally, she stops talking and watches, too. Everybody knows what's inside those big trucks. They're carrying all the equipment for the Fall Festival. The drivers will spend all afternoon and all night building booths, putting up rides, setting up the stage for the Battle of the Bands, and making sure the Clydesdales are settled in a nice warm stable that the workers will put together.

I'm still floating on a cloud from this awesome morning when lunchtime comes. Standing in the back of the line with Lisa McKinley is okay with me. I've learned how to keep a tissue close by, and when I see her take a deep breath, I cover up. It works for both of us. And now, Connie stands with me.

We're almost to the lunch counter when Nugget comes up behind us.

"Mya, I need you and Connie to meet me at the basketball courts at recess."

"I don't do recess," says Connie.

He frowns. "I need you to do recess today," he says, and walks away.

Connie and I watch him take a seat next to Fish. There are no smiles or talking going on between them. Something's wrong.

"I don't want to go to recess, Mya."

"I don't either, with Nugget acting like that. But he wouldn't ask unless it was important. Maybe you can come out for just a minute or two to see what's going on."

She nods. "I can do that."

After lunch, Connie and I look for my brother. He's waving his arms like crazy. Fish is with him.

So is Solo.

I don't want any trouble. If Nugget expects me to take up for him, or if he wants me to referee a wrestling match or something, I'm not doing it. Connie and I reach the guys and stop.

Nugget faces Solo. "Go ahead. We're waiting."

Solo walks over to Connie and me. "Yo, Connie, Mya, you're not losers." He turns to my brother. "Is that good enough?"

My brother nods, and Solo walks off to another group of boys. Nugget gives Fish a fist bump. I've got to know what happened.

Nugget shrugs. "The more I thought about it, the madder I got. It's one thing for him and me to have a deal. But it's a whole different thing for him to call my sister and her friend names. So I waited for him in the restroom. He's in there every morning, combing his hair."

I frown. "Nugget, you didn't start a fight."

"No, I didn't. But I told him if he didn't apologize to you and Connie at recess, I would beat him down and call him names he'd have to look up in the dictionary. He tried to man up on me, but I stood there with my fists balled. He backed down first, and said he'd apologize if I didn't tell everybody that he did."

"Told you he wasn't boo-yang cool," says Fish.

"You were right," says Nugget.

I spot Naomi and the twins, watching us. It doesn't hurt anymore to see them. I've got a really good best friend now. And I know she likes me for me. While I'm standing there, Connie moves closer to my brother.

"I can't believe you took up for me. Thanks, Nugget. You're pretty awesome."

He blushes. "Just call me Golden Nugget."

"Hey!" I say.

He laughs. "See you later. Fish and I have baseballs to catch before recess is over."

Connie and I walk around the playground, and I enjoy every step. Kids aren't staring at us like they used to. Twice we hear *Mya Tibbs Fibs* and *Mean Connie Tate*, but we keep walking. I guess I just don't care what people say anymore.

When Mrs. Davis blows the whistle for us to line up, I know it's time for the assembly. Instead of going back to our class, she has us sit on the floor in the cafeteria. The tables are all folded and stacked against the wall. The floor shines from a fresh mopping. Connie and I sit next to each other.

Kindergarten classes come in and sit up front. First graders are behind them, followed by second and third graders. We're close to the back wall facing the stage, and the fifth graders are behind us.

Soon, Mr. Winky climbs the steps to the stage and grabs the microphone.

"I realize we're all very excited," he says. "Fall Festival is by far one of the biggest events of the year. It is with great pleasure that I hold up this envelope with tickets enclosed for the Spirit Week partners who received the most points, including points from the cubby or cabinet decoration today. I'll start with the kindergarten classes and move up to our fifth graders. If I call your name, please come forward to claim your VIP tickets."

When Mr. Winky calls the two kindergarteners, the whole kindergarten class stands and hugs the winners. The winners run to Mr. Winky, accept their tickets, and hug him, too! I can hear his *yes, yes, yes* above the crowd.

Next he calls the first-grade winners, then the second graders, followed by the third graders. As

I sit and listen to the winners freak out and run to get their tickets, I wish I had a shot at winning, or at least Connie had a shot.

"And now our fourth-grade winners: Johnny Collins and David Abrahms."

Even though I knew we weren't going to win, it still hurts to hear someone else's name called. I wanted those tickets. So did Connie. We could have been the winners. There's no doubt in my mind that Animasia and Queen Angelica would have taken the five points on Thursday. What Connie did to our cabinets would have sealed the win for us.

"I'm sorry, Connie," I say.

She smiles and nods. "I know. Let it go."

Skye turns to Naomi. "Maybe you'll win next year."

"But definitely not this year," says Starr.

Naomi's glaring at me, so I look the other way.

Mr. Winky holds up the last envelope. "And the last two tickets go to: Fish Leatherwood and Bobby Joe McKinley!"

When I hear Fish's name, I stand and jump as if I had won. "Yay, Fish! Woo-hoo!"

Connie does the same until Mrs. Davis makes us sit down. I'm happy for everybody who won, but I'm sad that I ruined my chance, and feel even worse that I ruined Connie's.

"I have something for a very special student," says Mr. Winky. "This student put in long hours, before and after school, to make sure we had great posters on the wall for Spirit Week. She also volunteered for every job and every activity to ensure Spirit Week would be a success. She's been working on making Spirit Week special for over a month now. Connie Tate, get up here!"

Connie's face looks redder than tomatoes as she stands and walks to the stage. The clapping starts off slowly, but then it picks up, and soon almost everybody is clapping. Someone even raises a hand and shouts, "Hail to Queen Angelica!"

Mr. Winky stands next to Connie with an envelope in one hand and his microphone in the other. "Connie, in appreciation for all of the work you did to make Spirit Week a success, the staff of Young Elementary School would like to present you with a Fall Festival VIP ticket! Congratulations."

Connie holds the envelope up as she walks back to her seat. Her face is still red as she hugs me. "I'll share it with you, Mya."

I nod, still clapping for her until I realize I'm the only one, so I stop. Mr. Winky finishes his Spirit Week speech, but while he's talking, I stare at Connie's envelope. For days I didn't think it'd matter, but right now, I'd give anything to have an envelope with a ticket inside. When the assembly is over, while standing in line to go back to class, I see Nugget coming toward me. "Hey, Mya, wait a minute!"

He hands me a brown paper bag. "I meant to give this to you before we got to school, but I forgot. See you after school."

He runs back to his class line. I open the bag, reach my hand inside, and pull out two red T-shirts with Tibbs's Farm and Ranch Store written across the front.

Connie stares at the shirts. "What are those for?"

I know exactly what they're for. I grin at Connie and shrug.

"Today, best friends are supposed to dress alike."

I hand Connie a T-shirt. We slip them on over our blouses.

"I have something else for you," says Connie.

She unzips her backpack and pulls out another bag. "This is the costume your mom made for me. I wanted to give it back. But there's also something else in there."

I open the bag and see my vest. I snatch it out and hold it up. There's a whole western scene painted on the front with coyotes, cacti, cowgirl hats, and boots.

"You did this?" I ask.

"Remember when I knocked you down and you were all upset because I got paint on your vest?"

"Duh," I say.

Connie grins. "I told you I wouldn't forget."

I roll my eyes. "I thought you meant you wouldn't forget to rip my lips off."

"Why would you think that?" asks Connie.

I glare at her. She glares at me. We say it together. "Naomi."

Connie stands beside me and we stare at the vest. "I really felt bad about that blue paint spot because you wear that vest, like, every day. I got it from your mom when I came over to try on the Angelica costume. Pretty sneaky, huh? Go ahead and put it on."

I fold the vest and put it back in the bag. "I like how I look right now."

Connie puts her arm around my shoulder. "So do I."

Chapter Twenty-Eight

It's Saturday morning, and in exactly four hours, the Fall Festival opens. In my gut, I know the rides are ready, the stage is built, the food is cooking, and the big tent is just waiting to be filled with rodeo fans. I'm up early because Nugget, Fish, Connie, and I made plans to catch the trolley on State Street so we could be the first kids in line for everything. Nugget and I made bowls of cereal for breakfast since Mom is still asleep, and also made snack bags for ourselves, Fish, and Connie while we wait for the festival gate to open.

I even braided my own hair.

Dad strolls in and takes a seat at the table. "I hate to be the bearer of bad news, but I need both of you at the store this morning. I had to rush-order more boots and belt buckles. I even sold out of the hat Buttercup was wearing! And I just got a text from Mr. Crabtree that he told his friends about my corn mix and what it's done for his cattle. Now, three more customers have ordered twenty-five bushels each for their livestock and want it by noon today. I've got to have some help, kids. And I've got a special customer coming."

Nugget stares at his Froot Loops. My bottom lip shakes.

"I know you had Fall Festival plans this morning. I promise I'll personally drive you to the front gate and buy your tickets when you finish."

"But Fish and Connie will be here any minute," I say.

"Give them a call and tell them you have to work," says Dad. "You can call them from the store when you finish."

I nod. Nugget nods, too. We both scoot back from the table.

Dad grabs our hands. "For what it's worth, I'm so glad I can count on the two of you."

"You can always count on us, Dad," says Nugget.

"Always," I say.

"Tell Connie and Fish that I'll swing around and pick them up, too, if they want to wait on you."

Nugget and I shuffle upstairs. I'm dragging, upset that I have to work this morning.

"What am I going to do now? Since I don't have a VIP ticket, I wanted to be at the Fall Festival early so I could be one of the first people in line for the Whipper-Snapper and the Plop-Drop. By the time I get there, the lines are going to be all the way to Oklahoma."

Nugget holds my shoulders and whispers. "I'll call Fish and break the bad news. You call Connie. Hurry up and get dressed, because we still have to wash our cereal bowls so Mom doesn't have to clean up after us. The sooner we get started at the store, the faster we'll be finished."

Thirty minutes later, when I open the front door, there on our steps sit Connie and Fish, laughing and talking. Connie's wearing her Tibbs's store T-shirt.

"I was already awake, so I thought I'd come and help you at the store," says Connie.

Fish stands up. "I know how long it takes to fill those bushels with your dad's corn mix. I've helped you before, remember? I can help you again."

I give Connie a big hug while Nugget finds Fish

a T-shirt. Dad grins when he sees the four of us dressed and ready to work.

"How about that! Looks like I doubled my help in less than an hour! Let's go!" We pile into Dad's truck. Inside the store, Connie and I open up boxes of boots and stock them on the shelves. Then we open up boxes of buckles and do the same thing. While we're working, I teach Connie a new verse to my song, while she adds a few things to the store display. Soon, there's lots of noise at the front of the store. People are pushing their way in, but there seems to be a bunch of cowboys holding people back.

Connie and I tiptoe down an aisle so we can get a better look.

I hear Dad's voice. "Thanks so much for coming. Right this way."

We run back to where we're supposed to be, and wait for Dad's special customer. I can hear the conversation between Dad and a lady.

"Mr. Tibbs," she says, "I was hoping you had a couple of extra workers here who could help me at the festival. One of my ranch hands is down with the flu and I'm short-handed."

"I wish I could, but I've got my children helping me because I'm short-handed, too."

Suddenly, the cowboys move. A woman dressed

in cowgirl gear stands in front of me.

It can't be. Jambalaya!

"Cowgirl Claire?"

She looks my way. "Mr. Tibbs, is this your daughter you were telling me about?"

I'm jumping up and down. "Oh my gosh! Connie! It's . . . it's . . . oh my gosh!"

Cowgirl Claire gives us hugs. "It's nice to meet both of you. Young lady, don't you have a brother? What's his name? Niblet?"

"Nugget!" I shout louder than I mean to.

Connie puts up her hand. "I'll go get him."

Everything on the inside of my body is jumping up and down, but the outside of my body is stuck. Dad's smiling at me. Cowgirl Claire puts her hands on her hips and smiles at me.

"Your father tells me you know how to rope a calf. Is that true?"

"Yes, ma'am! Let me show you!" I grab a rope, make a lasso, and twirl it around.

"Woo-hoo, young lady! That's a mighty fine loop you've got working there!"

Nugget, Fish, and Connie show up. Nugget's eyes widen.

"Greetings and salutations, Cowgirl—"

Before he can finish, I throw that loop at my

brother, and I get him on the first try. I've got his arms pinned to his sides as I run toward him.

He's hollering at me. "Mya! You better not—"

I bull-rush him, knock him down, and hog-tie him on the floor.

"One, two, three!"

I throw my hands in the air. "It's a new world record!"

Fish gives me a high five. "Way to go, Mya Papaya!"

Cowgirl Claire claps and whistles through her teeth. "Would you looky there! Untie Niblet before he starts to moo! Well, I've got to get going. It sure was nice meeting you folks."

I don't want her to leave. There's so many things I'd love to ask her, and tell her, but my brain has gone to sleep again. I wish I could take this no-good brain out of my head and . . .

The best idea I've had all week forms in my mind.

"Excuse me, Cowgirl Claire, I heard you telling my dad that you're short on help for the festival. My brother and I could help you. We help at the store all the time, and we're both really good with animals. Nugget works in the barn here, and I do a lot of stocking supplies . . . and I help my mom clean up the kitchen after dinner."

Dad walks over and puts his hand on my shoulder as he talks to Cowgirl Claire. "You know what? Mya's right. I don't think you'll find a better set of helpers in Bluebonnet. This is the team you're looking for, Cowgirl Claire. I'd bet my store on it."

I'm shaking like a rocket ready to blast off into space. Nugget stands beside me with his hands by his side like a soldier. Cowgirl Claire is staring at us from head to toe, as if she's thinking about what Dad and I said.

"Well, you sure know how to make a good lasso, missy. And Niblet, I could use some strong arms to help with my horses. Okay! Mya, Niblet, you're both hired!"

Connie and I jump, clap, and scream all over Dad's store. Cowgirl Claire chuckles.

"Calm down, girlies! You're going to need that energy for work! While you're getting yourselves together, let me tell you about your job, Mya. You and your brother have to ride with me to the festival so I can tell you about your responsibilities while I'm doing my act. You'll both get Cowgirl Claire Show All-Access Passes, which must stay around your neck so the Fall Festival workers will know you're part of my crew. That All-Access Pass will get you free food, and first dibs on all the rides, shows, and backstage privileges at the festival since you'll have limited time to enjoy them."

Connie takes my hand. "It's just like a VIP ticket, Mya!"

I take both of Connie's hands and jump up and down with her. "I'm going to work for Cowgirl Claire. She hired me! Did you hear her?"

I let go of Connie and give Cowgirl Claire a big hug, and she hugs me back. Then she looks me square in the eye.

"Get yourself together, missy. We've got work to do. Round everybody up, Niblet! You can bring your friends with you if you want. I've got a big RV out front, and there's plenty of room, but we've got to skedaddle on out of here."

I rush over and hug Dad as tight as I can. Nugget does, too.

"I love both of you so much," Dad says, and tries to give us money.

"We won't need that, Dad," I say. "Everything's free for us."

He winks. "I'll pick you up later tonight, when the festival closes for the day."

I reach into my pocket, pull out a gift, and give it to Connie.

"Here—I made this for you."

She takes the yellow bracelet and stares at the letters. BRFF.

"Mya, what does BRFF mean?"

I shrug. "When I was making our matching bracelets last night, I put the letters BFF on them, but then I got worried that you would think that meant Best Fake Friends so I changed it to BRFF for Best Real Friends Forever! Do you like it?"

She laughs and then slips it onto her wrist. "I love it. I'll wear it every day."

I put mine on, too. "Let's sing the song I taught you while we were working," I say.

"Okay," says Connie. I put my arm around Connie's neck. She puts her arm around mine and we sing at the top of our lungs.

"*Connie Tate and Mya Tibbs are best of friends.*
And they're hoping that their friendship never ends!
Connie paints just like Picasso,
Mya's awesome with a lasso,
Connie Tate and Mya Tibbs are best of friends!"

Acknowledgments

I thank God for giving me the gift of creative writing. I truly believe I have found my purpose in life.

Reggie, Phillip, and Joshua, your support has been unfailing, and I'm so thankful for "my guys."

A very special thank-you to my nieces, Sydney Mabray and La'Nique Allen, for their help and ideas. I love both of you very much.

Thank you, Juliet White, Tim Kane, Varsha Bajaj, and Laura Ruthven for your amazing questions and comments, and for reading and rereading Mya until she was just right!

I'm so thankful for all of my family and friends who encourage me, especially Barbara Scott, Christine Taylor-Butler, Donna Gephart, and Neal Shusterman.

Thank you, Alessandra Balzer and Donna Bray, for believing in me, and for the opportunity to give life to these voices in my head!

Kristin Rens, I'm overwhelmed by all that you give. Your guidance, ideas, patience, encouragement, friendship, and belief in my abilities are so golden to me. I will forever be grateful.

Lastly, I want to acknowledge my precious friend and agent, Jennifer Rofé. You are as magnificent and unique as Mya. Thanks for everything you do.

Turn the page for a sneak peek at

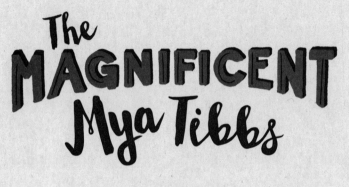

The
MAGNIFICENT
Mya Tibbs

THE
WALL OF
FAME
GAME

Chapter One

I push my cowgirl hat down on my head until it feels just right and then straighten my new outfit. I don't need anyone to tell me how boo-yang good I look in my new Annie Oakley skirt and vest. Mom made one for me and one for herself. Ever since kindergarten, we've worn matching outfits to Open House, and tonight, we're going to be the best-lookin' cowgirls on the planet! And as a bonus, I've got a folder full of A+ papers just sitting on my desk, waiting to make Mom holler "Yee-haw!"

But when I get downstairs, Mom is still in her robe, sitting on the sofa with Dad. I think you have to sit a lot when you have a little one in your belly. Mom's nine months pregnant with my baby sister, Macey, and she's always sitting, which proves my point. She said this October is the hottest one she remembers here in Bluebonnet. Maybe so, but if Mom doesn't hurry, we're going to be late to Open House.

I smile and twirl slowly so she can see how awesome I look. "I love this outfit and can't wait to see yours. You better get dressed. It's almost time to leave." Her face has a lot of sad in it. "I'm sorry, Mya. I won't be going to Open House tonight."

I stare at Mom, waiting for her to say something like "Just kidding!" or "Gotcha!" But she doesn't.

There is nothing worse than a bad surprise, and I just got one.

"But, Mom, you always go to Open House," I say.

"It's still hot outside, Macey's been kicking all day, and my stomach's sore. I hope you understand," she says.

I'm trying, but right now, the only thing I understand is that I made all of those good grades for nothing. At every Open House, Mom gives me super-duper hugs that make me feel good from my boots to my braids. That's not going to happen tonight.

My brother shuffles over and stands beside

me. His real name is Micah, but I call him Nugget because his skin is brown and his head is shaped like a chicken tender. He's wearing a T-shirt that reads *Does the Name Pavlov Ring a Bell?* It doesn't to me, but Nugget laughed out loud when he saw it at the children's science store.

"Sorry you're going to miss Open House, Mom," says Nugget.

She nods at him, "Me too."

Dad lowers his face to Mom's stomach and talks to it. "Macey? It's Daddy. What are you doing in there? Are you playing baseball?"

I clear my throat, even though there's nothing stuck in it. "Huh-*hmmmm*! So Dad, are you taking us to Open House? I don't want to be late."

He checks his watch. "Is it that time already? Let's go!"

Mom waves to me. "You're not upset with me, are you, Mya?"

I shuffle over and hug her with both arms. As Mom keeps rubbing her stomach, I'm thinking maybe it's good she's not coming with us. If Macey's kicking because she's trying to find the exit door out of Mom's belly, I don't want her poppin' out during Open House.

So tonight, it will just be Dad, Nugget, and me.

That's not as fun as having Mom with us. Dad fist bumps, and my As are super-duper hug As, not fist-bump As.

On our way to Open House, the heels of my pretty pink boots make a *ka-clunk* sound when they touch the sidewalk. They're supposed to, because that's how real cowgirl boots sound. We walk and talk about Open House until Nugget changes the subject.

"Dad, did you see the pitching line-up for game one of the World Series? The Yankees are throwing Wicked Willie Combs."

Dad puts his arm around Nugget's shoulder. "The Cardinals are going to have a hard time hitting Wicked Willie's curveball."

I keep walking, hoping this conversation doesn't last too much longer, because I don't know much about baseball.

Nugget kicks a rock off the sidewalk. "I've been studying his pitches. Now I can tell what Willie's going to throw before the announcer calls it. It's all in his arm motion," he says.

Dad chuckles and shakes his head. "Son, you're a baseball genius! I've never met anyone who can pick up baseball facts like you do."

I tug on Dad's shirt sleeve. "Excuse me, but we're

on our way to Open House, not the ballpark."

Dad's eyes widen as he smiles. "Yes, ma'am!"

As we get closer, cars and trucks line the street in front of Young Elementary School. Little kids run in the grass as groups of grown-ups talk and laugh under the streetlights.

"Hey, Nugget, wait up!"

It's Fish Leatherwood and his dad. Fish is my brother's best friend. His real name is Homer because his dad loves baseball, but Fish looks more like a boy than a home run. It's his big blue eyes that got him the nickname Fish. I can only look at them for so long, and then I get dizzy. Tonight he's wearing a T-shirt that reads *Either You Like Bacon or You're Wrong.*

As our dads shake hands and talk, Fish gives Nugget a fist bump and then turns my way. "Hiya, Mya Papaya!"

I love when he calls me Mya Papaya. It's not a good western name like Annie Oakley, but I still like it. "Thanks, Fish. I like bacon," I say, and point to his shirt.

"Me too," he says.

I add some giddy-up to my walk when I see Principal Winky at the front door. He's dressed in a blue suit and white shirt. Those are our school colors! He waves and gives us a big Texas-sized smile.

"Here comes my favorite plate of Fish Nuggets and a Texas cowgirl! Yee-haw! It's Open House, and we're going to have a wonderful evening at Y.E.S. Yes, yes, yes! Please take a program off the table on your way inside. Classrooms will open in thirty minutes. Until then, there are lots of things to enjoy, like refreshments and face painting in the cafeteria, picture taking for a good cause near the library, and of course, catching up with your neighbors. Have a wonderful time, yes, yes, yes!"

"Let's go get some punch," says Dad.

"We'll see y'all in Fish and Nugget's Open House," says Mr. Leatherwood.

Fish nudges me. "I bet Mrs. Davis talks about the Wall of Fame Game tonight. That's what she did last year when Nugget and I were in her class. Don't forget to sign up for it."

The smile slides off my face. "I'm not signing up for the Wall of Fame Game. Annie Oakley's movie marathon starts next week. Mom and I already have plans to watch it. I just need to get my folder and take it home so Mom can see it."

"Oh, okay, that sounds like fun," says Fish. "See you later, Mya Papaya."

I guess Fish doesn't check the TV Guide, or else

he'd know that Annie Oakley's movie marathon starts on Monday, the same day the Wall of Fame Game begins, and there's no way I can do both. Mom and I already made big-time plans to watch Annie Oakley. And if I signed up for the Wall of Fame Game, I'd have to study from the time I got home from school until I went to bed. Good gravy. Why would anybody want to do that?

I'm not making my brain do any extra remembering, and that's what the Wall of Fame Game makes everybody do. The truth is, this Wall of Fame Game isn't really a game at all. It makes kids study a bunch of boring facts when we could be having boot-scootin', loud-hootin' fun.

I know a dirty rotten trap when I see one. And I'm not falling for it.

the Wall Of Fame

Chapter Two

This has to be a record-breaking crowd for Open House! It's so loud in the cafeteria that at first I have to cover my ears. Voices echo off the walls as people stand around talking and holding cups filled with punch and little snack plates. If we were this noisy during lunch, Mrs. Davis would stand on the stage, hold up two fingers, grab the microphone, and count to five—that means zip your lip. But I don't think that's going to happen tonight.

There are two refreshment tables against the back wall. One has fancy bowls filled with red and blue punch. The other has cookies, cakes, and three big veggie trays with ranch dressing. On the other side of the cafeteria, there's a long line of kids waiting to get their faces painted. As I *ka-clunk* over to the veggies, I spot my best friend, Connie, and her little brother, Clayton, standing next to their mom.

I run to them as if we haven't seen each other in weeks, even though I just saw Connie in school a few hours ago. "Hi, Mrs. Tate. Hi, Clayton. Hi, Connie."

Both Mrs. Tate and Clayton hug me. Connie and I grab little plates and fill them with carrot and celery sticks and a glob of ranch dressing, and then shuffle back to the hall.

"It's kind of creepy being in school at night, isn't it? Where's your mom?" asks Connie.

This feels like the perfect time to tell a taradiddle. That's cowgirl talk for a story. I put my plate down on the table with flyers about Open House, hold both edges of my vest, and look as serious as I can.

"Mom's surfing the Nile, Amazon, and Mississippi, trying to set a record as the only pregnant woman to catch a wave on the three longest rivers in the world."

Connie laughs and rolls her eyes. "You and those taradiddles. And I don't think you surf rivers. You surf oceans."

I pick up my plate and sweep a carrot stick through the puddle of ranch dressing. "Well, it's true what I said about the rivers. They're the longest ones."

Connie and I both chomp down on the veggies. Her head tilts as she chews.

"Geez, Mya, how do you remember that stuff?"

I smile. "Every taradiddle a cowgirl tells has some facts in it!"

Connie nudges me with her elbow. "Speaking of remembering stuff, are you signing up for the Wall of Fame Game? You should. I bet you'd make the wall. The way you hold on to facts, it would be easy as cake. We could sign up together!"

I flip my wrist at her. "No way. There's an Annie Oakley marathon starting on Monday. It's kind of a big deal for Mom and me. We wear our cowgirl hats, eat popcorn, chew beef jerky, and drink lots of root beer. Dad even brings Buttercup into the house. When Annie chases the bad guys, Dad puts me on Buttercup and I pretend I'm riding with Annie to catch them!"

Buttercup is our mechanical bull. Everybody

from bullriding beginners to cow-ropin' profes-
sionals like to climb on his back for a spin. I'm not
afraid to ride him, but only on level one.

"I saw a commercial for the marathon on the
western channel. I bet you and your mom have a
bunch of fun," says Connie.

I grab a celery stick from my plate. "After that,
Mom and I have to get ready for the chili cook-off
next week. Cowgirls first, chili second. I can't wait!
Look out, Annie Oakley, 'cause here I come! Yee-
haw!"

There's lots of noise coming from the hall by the
library, so we make our way to the front, and find
Starr and Skye Falling, smiling and greeting people. On the other side of them is Naomi Jackson, my
old best friend, and her parents, looking proud and
happy.

Skye holds up her camera. "We're helping Naomi.
For a small donation, you can get your picture taken
with her dressed up as Junior Miss Lone Star."

Naomi's wearing a white pageant gown, a blue
sash across her shoulder that reads *Junior Miss
Lone Star*, and of course, her shiny tiara.

"She's charging money to get a picture taken
with her?" asks Connie.

I shake my head. "I can't believe it."

Skye nods. "All the money goes to the homeless shelter. You want to get a picture taken with her?"

Connie frowns. So do I. Naomi is the one who gave both of us our terrible nicknames—Mya Tibbs Fibbs and Mean Connie Tate.

It's been three weeks since I lassoed Naomi in the hall during Spirit Week. I remember like it was yesterday. Connie and I had just become friends, while Naomi and I dropped from BFFs to worst enemies. So when I had spotted Naomi leading a stampede of students toward Connie's art room, I'd thought she was going to trash it. I had to do something.

So I did.

Right there in front of my classmates, I lassoed her. In four seconds flat! I got in trouble for it, but I also set a new roping record.

I know she hasn't forgotten. I haven't, because it was one of the best roping days of my life. But I know she's going to try and get me back for that.

I take off my right boot, turn it upside down, and shake it over the donation bucket. Two quarters fall out.

"That's all I have. I don't want a picture with her, but I do want to help the homeless," I say.

Nugget and Fish race by on the way to their

classroom. Dad and Mr. Leatherwood wave at Naomi and her parents, and they wave back. That's when I notice Naomi watching me. She rolls her eyes. I roll mine back. Dad puts his hand on my shoulder.

"We're heading to Nugget's classroom, Mya. Meet us there in two minutes."

"Okay, Dad," I say.

Connie's mom waves as she leaves the cafeteria, holding Clayton's hand. He's got balloons painted on his face.

"Your little brother is so cute. I hope Macey makes people smile as much as he does," I say.

Connie sticks her tongue out at him. He laughs, and so does she. "Anyway, Mya, about the Wall of Fame Game—I'm definitely signing up. If I make it, I'll be the first Tate on the wall. Both my parents tried, but they missed two questions on the last day. I think they'd be really proud of me if I made it. Have you ever read all the names on the wall?"

I shake my head. "Every time I try, I lose my place and have to start over. There's so many names up there."

"I know! It looks like a thousand!" Connie walks toward our homeroom. "I bet your two minutes are up. You better get to Nugget's class before your dad comes looking for you. I'll see you in Mrs. Davis's room. We are going to have the best Open House."

I head in the opposite direction, toward the fifth-grade hall. "It's going to be a yippee-ki-yay kind of Open House, Connie! I can't wait!"

Don't miss these books by CRYSTAL ALLEN!